I0450791

ENTANGLED
WITH AN
ELF PRINCE

ENTANGLED WITH AN ELF PRINCE

Copyright © 2022 by Amanda Ferreira

All rights reserved. Neither this book, nor any parts within it may be sold or reproduced in any form without permission.

This book is a work of fiction. The names, characters, and events in this book are the products of the author's imagination and are used fictitiously. Any similarity to real persons living or dead is coincidental and not intended by the author.

Cover art by Reid Aster at kollapsart.com

Typography by Ren Tachibana at rentachibanaworks.com

Interior formatting by Leslie Copeland

ARC formatting by Elizabeth S. Trafalgar

First edition: October 2022

ISBN 9781778217401 (ebook)

ISBN 9781778217418 (paperback)

To all those who believed in my dream.

I could recognize him by touch alone, by smell; I would know him blind, by the way his breaths came and his feet struck the earth. I would know him in death, at the end of the world.

- Madeline Miller, *The Song Of Achilles*

CHAPTER ONE

I woke up suddenly to the sound of soft rain, aching in all the wrong places from a dream I'd had about Bren.

Blinking back sleep, I grasped immediately in the dark for my two swords, finding the hilts cold and heavy in my hands, but useless. Even as I kicked off my bedroll, turning over in my tent, I couldn't distance myself from the ghost of my best friend in bed with me, his breath on my collarbone, his hips between my legs. He was everything, everywhere, all at once—in the shadows, in my head, against my hands, against my *body*. Even with my eyes shut tight, my ears ringing, my thoughts distracted, the flurry of feelings remained. And with them came a deep, uncomfortable sense of awareness.

Because there, outside my tent—less than ten feet away —was Bren himself, his silhouette turned towards me in the dark, his broad shoulders and fine features like something out of a painting.

"Seven gods, Keenyn," he said quietly, the words slipping along the forest floor and into my tent like a tendril of mist. "Any louder and you'll wake the recruits."

1

At the sound of his voice, I heard one of those same recruits—the young elven boy who was supposed to be keeping watch with him—jerk suddenly in place, his body flailing in the night, his sword clattering onto the grass. Then, in the hush that followed, the boy muttered something about having closed his eyes for only a moment.

"For all the help you've been," Bren replied, "you might as well sleep in earnest. Go. Keenyn will lend me his company in your place."

There was another awkward beat of silence, and in it I hurried to dress, aware that Bren was expecting me. Waiting. Eager. Like he'd been in my dream.

Here? he'd wanted to know, his lips against my skin, over my pulse. I was sensitive there, and he'd found that out by accident, nearly a year ago, when he'd grazed his thumb across a growing bruise below my jaw. *Or is that too much?*

I couldn't stop it—stop the tremours, the sensations, from wracking my body. For every belt I tightened, every tie on my armour I fastened, the memory of Bren's hands haunted me. With every shift of my body, every shuffle of my clothes, details of the dream came back to me, vibrant and clear.

Do you want me to stop? he'd murmured, his hips in my hands, my knees on either side of his waist. *If you do, you'll have to tell me.*

Of course, my breathless response was how I'd ended up in this mess. *No. This is everything I want,* I'd told him.

Everything? I wondered now, hurrying to pull on my boots, the leather straps at my waist and my thigh going taut with a tug. *Surely my definition of everything would include—*

With a start, I heard Bren sigh and get to his feet, the

sound of his footfalls drowning out the recruit's as the younger boy headed to bed.

"Don't take your time, princess," he mumbled, my tent shaking as he knocked on the poles. But in his carelessness, one of them snapped under his knuckles, then another, leaving the canvas to collapse in on one side.

Affronted, but mostly surprised, I stuck my head out of the tent—only to find Bren's face less than a foot from mine, an apology wrapped in the soft curves of his lips.

It was too much, too soon. His piercing blue eyes, furrowed brow...

"If you insist on using my formal title," I said quickly, as sound rushed back into my ears, "the least you could do is give me some personal space."

At that, Bren snorted, leaning closer just to annoy me, his golden hair falling into his eyes. "Is that so?" he said, his voice low, his tone husky. And for a moment, I thought the sight of him smirking might kill me.

"Bren," I said carefully, trying to sound exasperated, but already, he was straightening up from where he'd attempted to right the broken poles.

The real advantage to mocking him was forcing some semblance of distance between us, so I wouldn't have to see his mouth in the moonlight or watch how his expression softened when he looked at me, his eyes trailing over the state of my hair. I couldn't bear it—not when I could hardly keep myself from imagining his lips on mine, his fingers tight around my wrists.

"I'll be right out," I said, glancing away from him, but by then, Bren had stalked back toward the trees, his shadow retreating from where it had lingered in my bedroll as if he'd only just risen from sleep and turned away.

Shaken, I dropped my gaze to my hands and slipped the

sheaths of both my blades across my back, crossing them where they met my hip on either side of my belt. I had nothing else to drag from the darkness of the tent save my breakfast, which was wrapped in a square of white cloth. Still, I took it, and when I sat down next to Bren near the outskirts of our camp, I offered him the bundle without looking.

"If you insist," he said, but after a quick count of the berries he stifled a laugh, his hand suddenly closing over mine, his fingers warm against my palm. "On second thought, you keep them. I'm not carrying you to Warrenhall if you collapse from hunger again."

Again. That was another memory I tried not to think about, especially now.

"You worry too much," I said, forcing myself to laugh, but after the night I'd had, even this small act of kindness from him made heat spread throughout my body.

Smiling now, Bren looked away, his attention darting forward as we both watched the forest, our sheltered glade ringed by trees that had grown so close together that ambushing us from behind was almost impossible. Still, I used any excuse to turn around on occasion, watching the leaves and the undergrowth for signs of movement.

But I had another reason for turning, whether I wanted to admit it or not. And each time, I found myself staring at Bren's side profile like I'd never seen him before—like his square face, bold nose, and strong jaw were completely new to me, as opposed to achingly familiar.

Seeing him like this, I realized I'd never thought of Bren as handsome before; it simply wasn't something I'd paid attention to. But in his full battle regalia, his breastplate glinting in the predawn light, his face sporting an early dusting of a beard, his shoulders broad enough for two men,

I almost considered it. He was obviously an attractive man, as far as humans went.

Fuck. What am I doing? I thought, but it was too late—Bren had caught me staring. With a slight turn of his head, our gazes met, and we looked at each other in that middle place between questioning and curiosity, pointed and patient. Then his expression turned vacant, like he'd rather do anything other than speak to me.

"You overheard the recruit earlier," he said, his voice flat. "It's what woke you. Why you're looking at me like that."

The non-question startled me. I had no idea what he was talking about. "What did the recruit say?"

To my chagrin, Bren thought I was being sarcastic. "You've met my father," he said, his expression pained. "You know it's just a rumour. It has to be."

Knowing there was only one rumour that had dogged Bren for most of his life, I puzzled out his meaning. "What, they asked if you were an unkillable god?"

On the surface, such a story was obviously untrue—or should've been, even to the wide-eyed boys we travelled with. But to their credit, to ignore the tiny fragments of truth—Bren's godlike physical strength; his impossible, unending endurance; the whispers of his father's fragmented memory of the woman he'd briefly loved—was a fool's errand. Divine or not, Bren was extraordinary, and to forget that was to get your leg broken when he tapped lightly on your knee.

"I know you're not, for what it's worth," I said plainly, turning my attention back to the woods. Above us, the sky rumbled with delayed fury, but the rain only lightened, the wind suddenly dying down. "I've seen you naked as a babe. You're as human as they come."

That, of course, was the wrong thing to say, but I couldn't take it back now, and the image of Bren's glorious body, carved like an offering to the gods, had not yet left my mind. If I'd been any less composed, I might've blushed.

Thankfully, Bren took the comment without blinking, assuming again that I was mocking him. "You're as bad as they are," he said, jerking his thumb at the tents pitched behind us. There were five recruits in total, none of whom treated Bren like another random monster hunter hired to cart them from one city to another. If he said *jump*, they half expected he'd give them the ability to fly. "Be serious for a moment, Keenyn."

I regarded him, slowly and carefully, watching as the tension on his face eventually split into a small smile. I was annoying him, that much was clear, but his frustration often led to a laugh; it was how we'd survived so many jobs together over the years.

"Yeah, all right," I said, dragging my eyes away from his lips again. "I was being truthful before; I didn't hear what the recruit said to you. You'll have to tell me."

In response, Bren reached out and touched my leg, fiddling with the hilt of the dagger on my thigh. I assumed it was an unconscious thought, automatic, the result of nervous energy flaring up in his hands. But in the wake of my dream, the sudden contact made my breath catch.

"He asked if you could kill me," Bren said softly, drawing the dagger now, holding the sharpened point beneath my chin. He paused then, before raising the blade and tapping the bone there, tipping my face up toward him.

"He's eight," I replied, taking the dagger from Bren's hand instead of directly answering his question. "Of course he wants to know who'd win in a fight between us. Farmers at roadside taverns place bets on worse odds."

I'd expected Bren to snort again, but his reply was strange. Loaded. Guarded. "He's worried I'll turn into a monster," he said, gesturing out into the forest, beyond our view. By now, the rotting deadwood mists were slipping away with the sun, so far from us they might as well have never been there at all. "I guess I've never really thought about it like that."

To avoid looking at him again, afraid of what my expression would give away, I pulled a length of woven cord from around my wrist, using it to tie back my hair into a top knot. But as I did, I remembered that Bren had been the one to buy it for me, and my cheeks warmed. The gift had been a small surprise after we'd run into a merchant on our way out of town. "Thought about what? Dying in the mists?"

"No," Bren said, his voice a whisper now, so quiet I had to lean closer to hear him. "What happens after. Would you be able to stop me, whatever I became?"

Spelled out like that, I could hardly swallow down my shock. "Bren," I said, shifting in the grass as I pushed out my legs, the heels of my boots driving streaks into the mud, "that would never happen. I'm always here. I would never let the mists get near you."

Abruptly—even before my answer was fully out of my mouth—Bren busied himself with getting to his feet, the back of his trousers stained from the long hours he'd spent sitting in the dirt and debating the possibility of his own death. For such a troubling line of thought, he seemed unbothered now, if vaguely annoyed.

"You're of no help," he said, speaking into the air above my head, directing his words at no one. "Pack up, then. The sun's bright enough; we should set out." And with that, saying nothing else, he turned, and I watched him go.

7

CHAPTER TWO

In my dream, *hold on* was the last thing Bren had said to me, the words breathed out like a prophecy, the closeness of his mouth pinning me down. I'd felt excitement then, as his hands roamed my body, but only a surge of anxiety now, the same words said aloud carrying a threat, a hint of danger. A warning.

"Hold on," Bren said softly, and I shivered, the reaction involuntary. "Do you see it?"

"See what?" I whispered back, but he'd already side-stepped in front of me, drawing his sword and slowing our horse, his hand on the animal's flank. The rest was automatic, honed after a long week on the road; I reached for one of my swords as the young elven recruits fell into formation behind me, the boys moving as Bren moved, wary but unafraid. As one, their attention lanced forward into the trees, searching for any sign of life.

"Can any of you see it?" one of them whispered, drawing a longbow and nocking an arrow, aiming into the distance.

In response, I touched the back of Bren's arm, nudging

him gently to the right so I could stand beside him, his shoulders pulled from my view. Ahead of us, in the direction of the rising sun, I saw low-hanging branches bunching together like children would, blocking the way. I shaded my eyes, but still, I saw nothing. There was overgrown greenery and the occasional yellow-breasted bird, but little else. "Where, Bren?" I asked, and he sighed.

"There," he said, and he leaned closer to me, nudging my cheek and tilting my head before pointing, his finger holding steady at some distant spot. I squinted, shifting in place—and finally, *there*, I could just see a vague, inky shape crouched low between two trees, the bend in its back cresting high above the undergrowth, its body little more than the impression of arms and legs. If it had a head, I couldn't see it; at least, not from our elevated position on the road.

"Maybe it's sleeping?" one of the recruits suggested, turning the pummel of his sword over in his hand. He couldn't have been older than fifteen, if that, and already, a life spent hunting monsters seemed to suit him, his features drawn tight with adrenaline. "We might be able to sneak up behind it, if we're quiet. Or we could slip past it."

His enthusiasm aside, the latter was sage advice. And knowing there were children among the group of recruits as young as eight or nine, I almost considered it. But we were also less than half a day's ride from the walls of Warrenhall, and the outpost was a newer one, built mostly from wood. To leave a creature this size so close to the front gate was much the same as asking someone else to fight—and die—in our place. And while Bren would never allow that, frankly, neither would I.

"Gather the younger boys between you," I instructed, gesturing farther back on the road. Together, three of the boys formed a loose ring around the others, their backs to the centre, their weapons in their hands. "Watch the horse, if you can. Watch the woods. And remember: never let one fight distract you from another."

Solemnly, the five of them nodded, and with that, I followed Bren off the road, between the trees.

Immediately, the oppressive quiet of the forest pressed down on us, muffling our steps and the sound of our breathing. The branches, jutting out randomly but consistently in our way, sloped down too close, rubbing leaves and shadows against our shoulders like war paint, the underbrush turning black in the lingering pockets of shade. It was all I could do to keep my eyes from being gouged out, while of course Bren muscled onwards like nothing could stop him.

For such a tall man, Bren could move as nimbly as any dancer, his steps light on the uneven forest floor, his footing steady. To stay behind him meant to mimic him, staying true to the path he cleared, my eyes aimed low in the shadows that twisted through the tree roots, watching his back and my own. In my hands, my twin blades were drawn, poised and ready.

"It's big," Bren said, stopping suddenly as we neared a large, grey boulder in our direct path forward. Moss-ridden, it shielded us from view, and beyond, we could just see the top of the creature's shoulders, its body doubled over, its arm emerging from the mess of green and brown surrounding it. Still, we saw no head, no hands, and no feet, as if every limb was purposefully hidden in the dirt. "Eight feet standing, I'd guess. Can you get behind it?"

Nodding, I chanced a quick glance back the way we'd come, just to see if the recruits were still all right. But by now, they were gone, hidden by the closeness of the trees and the thickness of the branches that surrounded us. It was a testament to Bren's keen eye that we'd managed to see any of the monster from the road, let alone enough to gauge its size.

"I'll try," I said in reply, but as I readied myself to pass him, Bren caught my wrist.

We were standing nearly flush, so close I could see the place where he'd just bitten his lip, the impression of his teeth disappearing as I watched. When I looked up, meeting his eyes, he hesitated before speaking, then leaned forward to press our foreheads together.

"I'll wake it," he said. "Don't provoke it. Don't get any fancy ideas."

I glanced away. "You're the hero," I replied, and suddenly I felt dangerously exposed, like he could read through the slight tremor in my hands and the fervent, desperate way my eyes dropped, again and again, to the corners of his mouth, and guess what it meant. What I'd dreamed. It made me uneasy.

Stepping back, I bent my body a bit lower for cover, then slipped behind the boulder shielding us, circling it until the trees gave way to a small, open glade.

From this side, the monster was no bigger—just rounder, like it had folded in on itself. And it never stirred, not even as I moved behind it, the view remaining unchanged save for the pile of dirt that appeared to have risen up against its back, partially burying it.

Thinking, perhaps, that it had died, its body long since entombed by the forest and the moss, I glanced up through the gaps between the trees and motioned to Bren, my sword glinting in the sunlight. He nodded back, but the movement was so quick I worried he'd mistaken my meaning.

To be sure, I stepped closer, just to better make him out through the overgrowth.

Twenty paces away, Bren was up to his waist in greenery, like the ground was trying to swallow him. In his hand, his broadsword swung high in a wide arc, ready to strike, the pummel gleaming even at this distance in the sun.

I was halfway to leaping out and trying to stall him, when suddenly I heard the recruits shouting in the distance, the upward slope of the road carrying the sound down toward us. But surely they wouldn't risk waking—

Then, to my right, I saw a shadow pass in front of the sun. I twisted, just as Bren started jogging towards the creature's hunched shoulders, his broadsword pulling even farther back, his attention solely forward.

And there, in the air, I saw a massive hand reaching out toward me, the splay of its fingers wide enough to crush a merchant's cart.

Immediately, I rolled out of the way, just narrowly avoiding being crushed as the monster's palm collided with the spot where I'd been, the ground shuddering with the impact, my teeth jarring around an awkward cry that split the air.

But there was no mouth near the place where Bren had struck, his sword carving through the monster's other hand. Instead, what remained of its long fingers pulled back to reveal crooked stumps and broken knuckles, black blood pouring out of its wounds and filling its purple nails with grime.

Seven gods, I thought, looking up from where I'd thrown myself to follow the lines of its body back to its real shoulders and real head. It was—by some miracle—still buried in the dirt from the armpits down, but its face had risen out of the grass like an overturned root, and from here, with eyes the size of a knight's shield, its mouth large enough to swallow horses, I thought the creature had to be at least forty feet tall when standing.

Jerking back to my feet, I ran towards it, my blades angled down, the cutting edges ripping strips out of the creature's gangly arms. It shrieked again, the pitch so low it hurt my ears, but I kept slashing, careful to avoid the backswing of Bren's massive blade.

Stabbing its palm, I saw Bren run up on my other side and carve through the monster's wrist, severing its right hand from its arm just as its left elbow came crashing down on us from above. I could only knock us both out of the way, grabbing Bren from the side and throwing us closer to the creature's face, its lower body still struggling to break free from the trees that had grown above it, its shoulders bent back beneath the weight of the dirt.

"Go!" I said, pointing at its left ear, then made a charge for its right. As a head, it could only thrash and scream at us, its teeth the size of anvils, its tongue as thick and long as a skinned cow. If we could avoid its bite, we had this; we could win.

Crying now, its sunken, dark eyes—once human, once warm—flew wide open, veins the width of a man's hand throbbing with anger along its brow. Shaken, I dove beneath its searching hand again, this one still uninjured, and cut at its thumb, accidentally spraying myself in the face with blood. It burned, filling my nose and mouth, and in the chaos, I felt it grab my leg and break something.

The pain was horrific. It lacerated up through my knee and into my hips, my entire foot going numb and collapsing under my weight. I stabbed the creature again, but it wouldn't let me go; it just squeezed me tighter, ripping me off the ground and flinging me into the air.

I lost track of myself for a moment, my body moving

upwards, buffeted by the wind. Then I was falling, everything rushing up toward me. I hit a tree, felt the sting in the back of my head, saw the world go black. Then I was back on the ground, my body seizing, my lungs coughing up blood.

I'd lost perhaps a second or two, but in those moments, Bren had reached the creature's head. I watched as he sliced off an ear, then cut into its cheek, his blade sharper than an axe. He didn't need to be coordinated, just determined, skin and bone splitting beneath his strikes.

All the while, he was grinning, his expression valiant, triumphant, otherworldly. Beautiful.

Then he looked for me, just for a fraction of a second, and our eyes met. His expression contorted, and he immediately changed tactics, dashing back toward me through the trees, then turning to keep the monster's attention.

I was grateful for the diversion. With his body as a shield, blocking me from view, I turned onto my back, flaring the source of my magic deep within my chest. I could hear the creature's remaining hand thrashing desperately through the nearby branches, smashing into tree trunks and unearthing everything that had ever lived here. But I couldn't focus on it, couldn't care; I had turned myself inward, the effort colouring all the markings on both my forearms from silver to gold, the pattern wild, twisting, like tree roots.

And in my leg, in my foot, I felt everything shift back where it needed to be, the bones regrowing, the skin repairing itself.

It was over in a moment. But in that same moment, the searching hand had found me again, slipping around Bren's swinging blade and wide stance.

With enough force to almost break my nose, the creature's palm smothered my face and grabbed my chest, yanking me from the ground. The soil beneath me dropped away as its fingers tightened, the creature crying out.

I didn't have time to think. I heard the monster's gnashing teeth drawing closer—I had to act.

With the markings on my arms still alight, I flared the magic hotter, angrier, crueler, twisting it from healing to destruction. My body immediately went cold, as if all my limbs had gone numb, my bones weightless. Reaching out, my arms around the monster's wrist, I poured magic into the gash I'd made on its thumb, ripping the wound apart instead of sewing it back together.

Screeching, the creature tried to drop me, but I held on. I could sense its arm like it was my own, every injury I'd inflicted seared into my mind's eye. I ripped them apart, one by one, stretching small cuts into deep slashes, shallow wounds into flayed skin.

It wasn't something I could keep up. I already felt the agony of what I'd lost, my fingers growing weak, my legs growing heavy, the magic exacting its cost. I dropped from its arm, landing hard, feeling my head spin. But with its hand torn open and the bones in its wrist exposed, Bren had no trouble cutting through it, then splitting apart its useless arm.

At last, the monster was little more than a writhing head, its mouth open, its eyes black and bloody. The sound it was making, halfway between a scream and a howl, had turned so inhuman that it was mostly noise, its pain and anger a physical thing tangling at our feet. In the long, singular breath before its death, I drew up beside Bren, tired and healed, but otherwise unhurt. He seemed unamused.

"A poor bounty," he said, moving behind it, and with a grunt, started hacking at its neck. With two strikes, its massive head dropped forward, its cries dying out abruptly. "Hardly worth your life."

I looked at him, his attention so distracted by the limbs in the dirt that he almost didn't hear my reply. "I didn't die," I said, then shook myself, as if that would help with the blood staining my clothes and the dull ache in my hands. "We're no worse for wear."

Bren shook his head at that, then ripped out two of the creature's teeth, using his sword like a shovel, angling the blade into the monster's dark blue gums. As he did, he actually smiled at me, his expression softening. "Still, I told you not to provoke it," he said. "Would it kill you to listen to me for once?"

I took one of the bloody teeth from him, needing both hands to carry the weight of it. "Anything is possible," I replied, but knocked our shoulders together as we turned to leave, his sturdiness like stumbling drunk against a tree. The moment felt normal, the forest still and quiet again, but our closeness was not lost on me; I could feel the heat of his breath in my hair, his gaze lingering on my now-healed leg. "In any case," I said, "we managed. And that's what matters."

Bren nodded again, but like before, only smiled. Whatever else he was thinking—good or bad—he left unsaid, and we walked back toward the road.

CHAPTER THREE

With his hair matted, his lips stained, his armour dented, and his clothes torn, I was mildly amused to find Bren decidedly more attractive. Against the sunlight, against the trees, he was everything he'd been when I'd first met him and more—unstoppable, untouchable, invulnerable.

But then he took off his shirt.

Stripped to the waist, walking alongside our horse, Bren looked like a man who'd stepped out of a storybook, his shoulders splattered with blood, his lips pursed, his eyebrow raised. As he moved, all that kept me from staring—at his chest, at his arms, at his back—was how he worked with his hands, his fingers tracing the places on his breastplate where the monster had struck him, pressing flat the indents with his thumb.

Thinking him distracted, I drank him in, but when he met my eyes, I cleared my throat.

"You're covered in bruises," I rightly pointed out, and the truth of it was stark. His skin, normally pale beneath his breastplate and cloak, was pockmarked by black and blue bruising, his breathing slightly laboured as he walked.

"That tends to happen when something hard hits you," he chided, but as he rolled his shoulders, I saw discomfort flash across his face. "It's not where anyone can normally see."

Of course, he'd been the one to undress; if he hadn't, perhaps I wouldn't have known.

"When we stop tonight, I can help with that. With your armour," I tried to offer, but he waved away my concern with his hand. As he did, his bloody palm flashed into view, revealing a gash where the tooth he'd been carrying had cut his hand, explaining why he'd suggested we stow them both in our saddlebags.

"You're a fool," I said, tapping his wrist, aware that behind us, the recruits had jostled together. They always hoped we'd get into a fight. "If you'd suck up your pride for just a moment, I could heal you."

Of course, that only made Bren laugh. "Save your strength," was his reply, and with hardly a moment's effort, he was back in his armour, his cloak around his shoulders again, swallowing his bruised skin. "I'll be fine."

But I didn't believe him, and rarely did, when it came to how badly he was hurt. And by mid-day, Bren's pace had begun to lag, and from the shortness of his breath, he was clearly hiding something from me.

So, at my request, we stopped for a short rest by a curve in the road, the recruits sitting with their weapons drawn and their lunches in the grass beside their knees. Ahead of them, Bren and I stood with our backs to the trees, watching for movement, his weight shifting from foot to foot.

"I think something's following us," I whispered to him, leaning as close to his ear as I dared. The movement hid the look on my face as I told him a bold-faced lie. "Maybe we should wait to see if it'll pass."

Bren turned his head in reply, his jaw nearly colliding with my nose. Still, his shoulder brushed roughly against my chest, like a rock grazing skin. I felt raw, where he'd touched me. "You're a terrible liar," he whispered back, but he was smiling again. Looking twice through the trees around us, surveying the swing of the leaves and the press of the wind, he ducked his head. His mouth was even closer to my ear than mine had been to his. "Quickly, then. But don't do much."

It was more permission than he usually gave me, which I solemnly noted. "Do you want the recruits to see?" I asked, but he'd already raised both of my hands and pressed them to his cheeks, my pinkies against his throat.

"It'll be good for them," was all he said.

This was rarely something so intimate. Usually, Bren would allow me to place one of my hands on his chest, or perhaps directly over his injuries. In very rare cases, I would cradle his head, but only if he was bleeding out and lying on the ground. Once, I'd healed him while he slept, my hands wrapped tightly around him from behind, but it was something we'd never spoken of again.

Thinking of that now, I fought back a flush, thankful my skin was two tones darker than steel. Around us, the forest and the recruits seemed to hush, our closeness gaining its own sense of gravity.

"What are you doing?" I whispered, his hands over mine. His eyes were so blue I thought I might drown.

"Waiting for you," he said, his voice completely unbothered, unstrained. "I said quickly, remember?"

I shook my head, more as a reaction than anything else. It calmed me, but only slightly. "Close your eyes, then," I said.

Healing Bren always came naturally to me, as if my

magic responded to him in some unusual way. Perhaps he was truly part god, and that essence in his blood made the touch of my magic sing. Either way, as the markings on my arms glowed gold, filling the space around us with a pure, unbroken light, it was impossible not to see him as more than what he was.

Beneath my hands, I felt every inch of him, even the flicker of his breath, warm, in his chest. It was like he'd stepped inside my head, expanding my skin beyond the edges of my body. I sensed every ache, every pain, every sore spot he'd tried to hide. For a moment, he was me, and he was all I knew.

Reaching down, behind my ribs, I flared the magic hotter, then hotter still. It burned against my bones, eating away at the adrenaline that coursed through my heart. Then it dropped to my legs, bringing with it an onslaught of weakness, then numbness. It spread quickly, upwards, consuming my knees. My head felt lightweight and empty.

But Bren was healing, improving, and that was enough. In his chest, I lessened the bruises I had seen and the strains I had not. Then, in his hand, I pulled his skin back together.

When I was finished, I let him go. I stepped back.

"Better?" he asked softly, as if a sense of relief was all I'd paid for.

"Ask yourself that," I replied, and sat down in the dirt.

The demonstration had brought with it a sudden sense of awe, which was palpable now, as if the recruits had never seen magic before. As if their own arms, which had not yet been marked, never would be. "What did you do?" one of the older boys wanted to know. "Can he fly?"

"I've never seen someone fly," Bren replied, and to my chagrin, he made an effort to try. But jumping twice produced only an audible sigh from his lips. "I'm as disappointed as all of you."

"It's healing magic," I explained, but by then, their interest had waned. Amazing, what was considered entertainment on the road and for how long. "It's not— It still takes skill."

At that, Bren snorted, then sat down beside me, pulling me into the space on his right. "Don't beat yourself up," he said. "I know what you did. I can feel it. And I can still feel you."

I looked away. "That awareness will fade in a moment," I said, popping a crushed, sodden berry into my mouth. It tasted like linen. "Though you put on quite a show."

Again, Bren leaned forward, his lips near my ear. "You enjoyed it," he said, his voice low, his tone teasing. "One less scar for the guildmasters to complain about. That matters, I think you said."

My face burned. "Bren, you're a fool."

Smirking, he at last pulled back, reclining on his arms. "So you keep telling me."

Whatever his mood, Bren let it persist, and by nightfall he remained unbothered. It wasn't like him; the approach of darkness—and the mists—usually made him nervous, even skittish. But not tonight. He simply nodded at our horse, taking my hand. "You should ride," he said, loud enough for all the recruits to hear. "You look tired."

It was true, and I felt more tired than I let show. Between the fight and the magic I'd used, defending us, healing him, I could hardly keep my eyes open. "If you're sure—" I started to say, but he'd already slowed the horse, stalling our progress, and wouldn't move again until I clambered on.

Up in the saddle, the press of the shadows seemed farther away, and the mists farther still. But as the hours crawled by, the darkness crawled closer, until the mists all but encircled us, colouring the ground an eerie, muddy blue.

"Bren," I said, but he was already moving, careful to remain within a pace of me. On his other side, the recruits fanned out loosely, waving their hands to dispel the potency of the mists.

Dimly, somewhere ahead, I knew the outpost was coming—I could smell the fires from the evening's cooking carrying beyond the trees. But when we finally spotted its tall, wooden walls, Warrenhall was little more than an outline in the darkness, the moonlight failing to pierce the gloom.

"Can they see us from the guard towers?" I thought to ask, but Bren was already signalling from the road. He should've been impossible to make out, at this distance, but there was no mistaking him. No one cut against the trees like Bren, not in armour.

He put down his waving hand. "There's someone atop the wall," he replied. "They're alone, though. And that's troubling."

Warier now, we began our approach, stepping out from the overgrowth onto the hard, densely packed dirt that surrounded the outpost. They'd salted the land here, barring the way for anything to survive.

"There has to be others on watch," I said, but even at the gate, only one voice echoed out to hail us.

"Step back," they said, and with a grunt, long ropes tightened with an audible tautness, the large portcullis barring our way pulling up to reveal an even larger wooden door. Splitting down the middle without a sound, it opened, swinging inward.

Beyond, there was no light at all; just a whisper of a figure standing tall in the entryway. "We've been expecting you since early afternoon," she said, and in the darkness, I thought she might be elven, but it was so hard to tell. "Did you run into trouble?"

"There's always trouble," was my reply, and I gestured at the blood on my boots, on my arms, on my chest. "But all the new recruits for the hunters' guild are accounted for. I trust I can leave them with you?"

She was hesitant, her gaze turning upwards, as if loathe to leave her post, even at the request of her prince. "Surely you could—"

But then Bren cut in, his hand squeezing my leg. "We could use beds, baths, a warm meal. What can you spare?"

For all his charm, Bren carried himself with the kind of arrogance that would've gotten any lesser man into trouble. Still, the woman's expression softened, as if humbled he'd spoken to her at all.

"Anything for a god, I suppose," she said in elvish, and then beckoned us forward, motioning for the recruits to wait for her in the courtyard until she returned.

But Bren, holding back, waited until she'd stepped away to say, "Did she refuse?" And in the fading light, flickering from the small torch atop the wall, I was aware of the tremble in his hands. So I ruffled his hair, hoping to soothe him, and was rewarded with a small, unusual smile.

"She'll give you anything you want," I said. "Even though it's not her job. It's one of the perks of being you."

I pulled away, jostled by the distance our horse kept between us, but Bren caught my wrist, and for a moment, neither of us moved. Then, for a reason I didn't know and couldn't guess, he kissed my palm. Quickly, lightly, as if we both weren't covered in blood.

"Stay close," he whispered, my pulse spiking, my cheeks heating, my lungs forgetting how to breathe. "The mists are thick tonight."

CHAPTER FOUR

Having to bathe in a shared wooden tub, our bodies so close that our thighs brushed against each other's, was a unique kind of torture only made worse by Bren's obliviousness.

I'd had no reprieve today, not for an instant—Bren was always naked, smiling, or tipping up my chin, and even now, he somehow managed a magnificent combination of all three, his fingers curling delicately along my skin, tilting my head this way and that.

"You missed a spot," he said, his voice so intense and serious that even his smirk couldn't break the near-explosive tension between us. "I win, then. You're paying for our room and board."

"Prove it," I said, wrestling myself out of his hand. "You'd say that even if it wasn't true. And you were covered in less blood to begin with."

Grunting, Bren shrugged and leaned back instead of answering, the muscles in his chest flexing in the candle-light as he moved to sit across from me in the tub. "You're a sore loser," he said at last, but again, the slight upturn of his mouth hinted at amusement masked by his tone. "Still, at least you're cleaner. No reason to have you thrown from the city gates in the morning now."

"Surely they'd have let me walk out," I chided, but it felt wrong. Everything about this felt wrong. From how close we were sitting to how much he was smiling, I felt inexcusably out of place. How did bathing together raise no arguments? No complaints? When had he allowed us to grow so close?

At my snide comment, Bren shrugged again, and the scars along his shoulders pulled and puckered like snagged seams in a bolt of cloth. I couldn't help staring at the raised impressions as I always did, wondering what they hinted about his life before we'd met. And for once, he sated my curiosity.

"They're old, Keenyn," he said, sounding a bit exasperated. "You weren't there. It was a miracle anyone healed me before I bled out."

"Was it a monster?" I asked, trying to imagine something ripping through his armour and tearing into his flesh.

Bren frowned, then responded simply with, "No."

In the resulting pause, I ran into the only thing I thought might be possible. "Someone attacked you?"

"Tried to kill me, actually," he clarified. "Came the closest anyone's ever come."

Immediately, I mumbled, "That's impossible," the reaction so automatic the words hardly registered before they left my mouth.

"What?" Bren asked, raising his eyebrow, his expression darkening. "You don't think I'd be the target of someone's malice? Someone's jealousy? Anger?"

"No," I replied, speaking too soon, too quickly. "Just... you, almost dying? To a knife in the dark, no less? The world would have to end."

Bren's eyes widened in response, his body going still. His shock was something alive, so wild I could almost hold it in my hands.

Then, after a too-long pause, he said, "You know I'm not invulnerable, Keenyn."

In his moment's hesitation, so unexpected I felt my heart beat four times in agony, I changed what I'd been about to say. "It looks like a bad injury, I don't doubt that," I said. "And it must have—"

"Can you hear yourself?" he asked the room, his attention on the darkness. I followed his gaze, looking past the silhouettes and shadows, only to find the window that I'd boarded up myself, the two layers of wood and nails something the outpost guard had set aside for us.

"You're still thinking about this morning," I said, watching as his posture stiffened, his jaw set. Then, under his hand, the rim of the tub cracked and broke away.

Startled, Bren looked down; at the same time, I reached out.

With my hand over Bren's, I pried the piece of wood from his fist—no bigger than his palm—and dropped it onto the floor. I couldn't help him; not really. But realizing I'd been so absent today, so distracted, while he'd been struggling with genuine self-doubt, filled me with shame.

"You have nothing to worry about," I said softly.

In response, Bren's gaze slammed into mine, his expression so conflicted I felt the emotion like it was my own. Then he blinked, and his moment of rage drained out of him like a stolen breath.

"For someone so clever," he said flatly, still looking me dead in the eyes, "you can be an idiot sometimes."

Then he got out of the tub, so abruptly water splashed out over the side. I had no idea what I'd done wrong.

"Go to bed," Bren said loudly, his eyes on the window again. Was he afraid to see some tendril of the mists that weren't there? "It's late. And I'm tired of this."

I didn't need to be reprimanded twice. I dressed quickly, waiting for Bren to turn his head, then lay down quietly on the bare mattress next to his, watching as each of the small candles by the tub put themselves out in their own pools of wax. By then, I was almost completely sure he'd relaxed beneath his threadbare blanket.

"I'm touched you think I'm clever," I whispered, more to myself and the room than to Bren. "But the compliment really undercuts how pissed off you are."

And to my surprise, he was still conscious enough to swear at me in elvish.

Bren must have slept in until the hour before dawn, then slipped from his bed; it was the only explanation I had for why his sheets were cold when I found them, his pillow flat, and the mattress seemingly undisturbed. It was almost as if he'd never been there at all, but that couldn't be right—I'd spent half the night listening to him snore, his breaths as steady as a heartbeat. No, he'd simply left, his steps careful, his arms empty; he hadn't even taken his sword. If I weren't so annoyed, I'd be impressed he snuck past me, what with the creak and the clamour raised by the floor.

Of course, following after him was easy enough, now that the sun was up. But knowing he hadn't gone far— hadn't left Warrenhall's barracks at all, in fact—came with questions I didn't like answering, and one in particular that soured on my tongue like rotten fruit. Why had he wanted to be alone?

Headstrong, I thought. *Vengeful. Frustrated.* But the words suited him as poorly as our borrowed clothes, which we'd swiped from the drawers of empty rooms deeper in the barracks. He was a man made for silk and steel, my Bren.

Which explained why he'd decided to fight in them, in the large square of dead grass circled by the barracks' two-story walls, dirtying the rough-spun cotton. The courtyard was meant to be a training ground, framed by unstrung bows and cheaply made practise blades, but with Bren at its centre, it might've been an amphitheatre for all his specta-tors cared. Bare to the waist, he was sparring with a group of men who charged at him blindly, their blades swinging wildly, their attacks high and wide. And Bren, with his piercing eyes and flashing teeth, moved like a bear. Head down, shoulders back, he'd no sooner be outflanked by a common soldier than a god.

I didn't call out, didn't draw his attention, but I didn't need to; Bren met my eyes the moment my foot left the last of the stairs. The columns parted, and between his oppo-nents, his gaze pinned me like a butterfly beneath glass, his attention sharp.

"Keenyn!" he said loudly, then looked away, pivoting in place to kick an elven woman in the knee. She'd tried striking him in the side in a coordinated attack with two others, but together, they all fell in a heap. "Wonderful of you to join us at last."

With that, he stepped away from his ring of opponents, nodding at each of them as if their armour and effort had levelled the playing field. It had not.

"You're late," he teased, wiping his brow. "It's nearly midday."

I kept my eyes on his face, away from his scars. "Having fun?" I asked, gesturing vaguely at the carnage. Between all the guards he'd knocked on their backs, there was enough bloody noses and bruised pride to darken the soil. "Forgive me, I didn't mean to interrupt. Please, blow off steam as publicly as you need to."

Bren smiled, cocking his head, his expression as arrogant as ever. I liked this side of him; but then, I always had. The bravado suited the bold lines of his face. "We should spar, you and I," he said, smirking at my clothes. "We're both dressed for it, clearly."

At my scoff, Bren raised an eyebrow.

"I know you're not scared, not like them," he said. "So why run? Why not face me?"

I saw through him—through the act, well-worn and comforting. "This can wait," I replied, my eyes on the crowd, aware that whatever had been bothering him still weighed on him heavily. "You hardly slept. Why the show?"

He blinked. Calmed. Steadied. "Maybe you owe me one," he said, "for keeping me up."

I met his eyes, pulling my attention away from his chest, stepping closer. "Bren," I said, keeping my voice low, "you shattered my nose the last time we fought."

His laugh was husky. "And you dislocated my shoulder. You're the only person who's ever done that." Then he glanced up at me, his gaze lingering on my jaw, before he stepped away, putting distance between us. "Come on. Let me have this, Keenyn."

At the hint of pleading in his voice, I finally relented, and Bren fell back into a fighting stance, his knees apart, his arms braced in front of his face. He was bigger than me. Taller. Heavier. But as he adjusted his weight, shifting on his feet, I reminded myself that he was still my friend. That he was still someone I knew.

I'd be all right.

I glared at him and rolled my shoulders. "Not the face, please," I said, and Bren nodded.

Then he charged, head-first, elbows out, his hands in tight fists. It was like watching the point of a spear hurtling toward me.

I braced. And quickly, as he drew close, I sidestepped him. Stayed within reach. It was my only trick; to minimize the space between his fists and my hands.

I grabbed his wrist as my next move, twisting behind him, and ducked under his arm. Then, when he kicked out his leg, I jumped forward, vaulting over his head.

He was fast; Bren had always been fast. But I was faster. It gave me an edge over him, but only slightly—that, and knowing how he preferred to kill things. Which side he favoured. How his eyes moved before he struck.

He turned as I did, grabbing his other hand and swinging both toward me like a battering ram. I fell back, out of the way, and felt the air warp around his swing, hissing against his fists. Then I slid forward again and struck at his chest. He blocked, our forearms meeting, and my bones rattled. Then he thrust out his palm and hit me in the shoulder.

I was pushed onto the ground by the force of the strike, but twisted to avoid being pinned beneath his knees. I rolled once, then kicked out with both legs, catching him mid-lunge as he dove to grab me, flinging him aside. Already, I was winded. But Bren, a dozen fights in, seemed unperturbed.

On my feet again, I ran up behind him. He struck backwards, and only my reflexes saved me from taking his fist square to the ribs. Then Bren turned, curling his arm around me. My back hit his chest. If he slammed our heads together, I'd be dead in an instant.

I had to be faster. I jabbed one hand into his elbow, trying to break his grip, and his body heaved against mine, aware of the impact but unhurt. I dropped my weight, sliding out of his arms. He kneed me in the side as I escaped.

I felt the give in my chest as bones broke, the pain nearly enough to kill me. I healed myself immediately as I dodged another swing from his right arm, but my sharp intake of breath made him falter, his next swing going wide. The magic was bright and cold, shining through the sleeves of my shirt, in a golden burst as radiant as the sun.

I caught his next fist against mine, bruising my knuckles and all of my fingers. I never did this; facing him head-on was to beg for an injury. But I snapped out my other hand, catching him in the chin, and his teeth just clipped his lip as he turned away. I felt his blood beneath my fingers, wet and hot; saw him swallow. Then he smiled, genuinely, so wide it lit up his face.

An instant later, he had pushed me back, knocking my foot out from under me. I rolled to the left, but he grabbed my leg, forcing it aside as he pinned me down with his knee, flat on my back.

I could kick him in the groin, from where I was, or I could jab him in the eyes, blinding him. But I refused.

Instead, I wiggled away from one final punch, twisting as his fist hit the ground. But then he grabbed my upper arm and threw me back, holding it above my head, his chest an inch above mine. Roughly, he leaned over and knocked our foreheads together.

It dazed me. For a moment, all I could see were stars in my eyes, my body paralyzed, my head aching. Any harder and he'd have crushed me, broken bone. I flared my magic, warming my face, and waited for the pounding to stop.

"I yield," I breathed out, but Bren pressed his lips just above the corner of my mouth, stealing the words.

"Don't do that," he said, so quietly I hardly heard him. "You killed me. You won." Then he smiled again, so wide and so earnest I felt the earth shift on its axis. "But you got lucky."

I struggled against him, just to shift myself away from his face. From his lips. I'd never wanted to kiss anyone so badly in my life. He'd never made avoiding it so impossible.

"If you say so," I whispered back. But I knew it was true, that he was right; I had seen the cut on his lip, the stain on his teeth. Any amount of magic, turned angry in my hands, would've ripped his skin from ear to ear, and he'd have bled out in the dirt. I hadn't done it, but I could have, and that was the only truth that mattered. "Will you sleep easier now? Knowing I could kill you?"

Again, his laugh was husky. The sound made my body shake, and as he eased himself closer, his chest lying flush against mine, I wished—suddenly, desperately—that we were alone. That we had more time.

"It shouldn't be a comfort," he said softly. "But it is."

Then he pulled away, taking the heat of his body with him, his expression serious. He was hardly sweating, his breathing still perfectly even, his hair just barely in his eyes as he swept it away. It was as if nothing had happened, as if nothing had worried him.

It's you they'll remember, I thought, watching as he waved at the cheering crowd. It was always that way, no matter where we went and what we did.

"The day's ahead," he said at last, when he turned back to me and held out his hand. I had waited for the moment he'd spare—for the reminder he'd never forgotten me. And wouldn't. "If you turn in that creature's teeth for the reward and get our next assignment from the guild house, I'll find breakfast somewhere. My treat."

It was a simple thing, this arrangement between us. A sharing of glory, in a measure only we knew and only we could see. But it made me happy; gave me purpose. I owed him everything I'd become, in any case. Every day I'd lived past meeting him was all borrowed time.

"Wait for me," I said, and took his hand.

CHAPTER FIVE

My last thought before falling asleep, the taste of breakfast still warm on my tongue, was of Bren; of his eyes, piercing in the growing gloom of the rolling fog, his hands in my hair, my breath warming his knee. I'd only meant to shut my eyes for a moment—to rest on the awkward slope of the barracks' roof—but I awoke in our room, back in my bed, my pockets empty, and Bren gone again. That he'd carried me here, and that I'd slept soundly enough not to notice, was one thing, but finding his armour missing, his sword gone, and his borrowed clothes discarded, was another. The only thing worse was the smell carried in through the window, heavy with blood.

"Seven gods," I murmured, fumbling around in the darkness as I made my way to the door, my senses dull, my body slow. I'd expended more magic that morning healing my ribs than I'd realized, and I was still tired from the day before; it left me clumsy, uncoordinated, as I pushed out into the narrow hallway, half-expecting to see something waiting for me. But there was nothing; nothing horrid, nothing dark, nothing as wild and irregular as my pulse. Just the quiet.

Until, all at once, there was Bren.

Jaw set, eyes wide, he appeared so suddenly at the end of the hallway that I nearly mistook him for a shadow. But then the silver of his breastplate glinted in the darkness and cast his face in a somber glow. At his back, his sword rose high above his shoulder, his hand already halfway to the hilt. But when he saw me, he stilled, and the relief that came over his face made me shudder.

"Bren," I said, holding his attention as I moved closer, his eyes alight as he drank me in. He seemed calmer, now that I was in sight, and the Bren I knew—composed, restrained—came back to himself. "Are you all right? What's going on?"

His reply was soft. "The usual chaos," he said, and though his voice was measured, it was obvious how worried he'd been just a moment before. "There are bodies in the streets. I was just coming back to get you."

Our eyes met, then, and I might've laughed, but the sense of tragedy in the air kept me silent. "You let me sleep," I said, and as I drew within arm's reach of him, I punched him lightly in the chest. "That was stupid, by the way. I'll grab my swords."

But when I turned to head back to our room, Bren caught my hand, passing me a square of parchment. I looked down, surprised to see the assignment notice he'd taken from my pocket this morning, the seal broken, the paper torn.

"Forgive me," was all he said, and when I looked up at his face, I found his expression difficult to read.

"It's bad news," I said, even before I unfolded what

remained of the note. And it was, because our new job was only addressed to *me*.

Keenyn, it read, with a slash of ink where my last name should've been, as if my identity was as informal as the scrawl on this page—as if my father, and the legacy I'd abandoned, meant less than nothing while I was here, in the woods. *By order of the Lord Knight-Commander of the Queen's Legion, you must head north. You have been tasked with hunting down the beasts that have plagued Warrenhall for some weeks, which are spitting back the bones of innocents who—*

It trailed off abruptly, and I looked up from where Bren's thumb had clearly ripped through the page, leaving a crater where the rest of the missive should've been. Only a few scattered words remained, near where the guildmaster's seal had been pressed into the wax. "You're upset," I said plainly, and Bren laughed.

"You'd think he'd have the courtesy to address the note to me," he said, running his hand through his hair in irritation. "The *Lord Knight-Commander*. He could've just told me to stay out of it. Let you go. Come home."

"Your father," I said incredulously, "has never been direct about a damn thing. You know that."

"He's direct when it comes to you," Bren said, and for a moment, I saw a flash of the same memory that I was sure clouded his eyes. I saw the forest again, remembered the rain; heard the deal he'd made with his father—on the night we'd deserted from the Queen's army—to keep me alive, to stay the executioner's axe. *If you hurt him, you'll never see me again.*

"This is a suicide mission," Bren continued, his voice hard. "He expected you to read this, head north, and die."

"You thought I'd go?" I retorted, gesturing to the ruined

note. "Alone? You thought I'd read this and keep it from you?"

To my shock, Bren looked away. The conflict in his eyes, in how it settled around his mouth and furrowed his brow, made me hyperaware of how close we were standing. So close that the darkness hid nothing of his face, of his lips. Of the way his words shook when he swallowed.

"You're soft," he said carefully, his gaze on the wall to his right. "You have a good heart. The rest of the letter... made it clear the outpost needs help. And you always fall for that."

I crossed my arms. Into the quiet, I said, "I would never have gone without telling you."

"To protect me, you would have," he returned, and I knew he was right. Worse, *he* knew he was right. And likely, that was how his father had phrased it.

Head due north from the walls of Warrenhall, deep into the heart of the deadwood grove, where the mists rise less than an hour after sunset, where grown men die from a single rogue breath, where any lack of your attention would lead to the death of any human who accompanies you—

No. I shook my head, trying to rid myself of his father's voice. "We're a team. We would've discussed it, like we're discussing it now. And maybe we'll still decide to take the job, but I won't go without you. I wouldn't have."

Bren closed his eyes, drawing in a deep breath through his nose. He mussed his hair again, looking pensive, shutting me out. Then he sighed, shifting his weight from foot to foot.

"I was out there," he said. "Just now. The fog was so dense, the people next to me disappeared before I even realized we were under attack. Whatever they are, these monsters can fly. They're quick and they're deadly, and they'll kill everyone in this place unless we stop them."

"It should be us," I concluded, though I didn't like saying the words. Condemning us—condemning *him*.

"I'll meet you at the gate," he said finally, turning on his heel. "I'll pack the supplies, find our horse. You get dressed. We might be able to follow them back to some kind of nest if we hurry."

The matter sounded settled, and as Bren walked away, I almost let him go. But my thoughts took hold of me, forming between my teeth like a song.

"Bren," I said. "We don't have to do this."

He didn't turn around, but he did stop with his hand on the door, his back rigid, his posture stiff. I knew he'd heard the things I hadn't said.

After a moment, he nodded. "I'll see you at the gate," he repeated, and left without looking back.

Returning to our room, the beds cold again—as I pulled on my boots, the laces tangling in my hands—I thought back on what Bren had said, in the hallway, his eyes tracing the lines of my face. *You have a good heart.*

He'd used those words on purpose, echoing what he'd told me on the very first night we'd spent together in the rain. I hadn't even known his name, at the time; he'd just been my captain, the leader of the Queen's army, a man out of legend, untouchable, undefeatable.

Until he'd fallen, gasping, blood pouring from a savage slash to the throat.

I could still remember that initial flush of magic, bonding us. How his body had stilled beneath my hands, his eyes on mine, his lips parted as I leaned close, my expression wild and panicked. I'd never healed another person before, never felt closeness as I'd known it then. In that moment, he was me and I was him, every beat of his heart my own, every breath ripped from all four of our lungs.

He'd lived, of course, and I'd been reborn as something new. Something not wholly my own.

I don't know why I saved you, I'd said, in the aftermath. It had been a risk, to heal a man I hadn't known, and whose death would've ended the war.

In response, he'd lain down beside me, quiet beneath the trees, his bedroll propped up like a makeshift tent above our heads. It'd blocked nothing of the weather, but had hidden us from passing patrols, the crunch of other men's boots keeping us awake. *I think you do,* he'd said.

I'd turned, in time to see him smile, soft and wistful, and I'd been lost. *You have a good heart,* he'd said.

Thinking back on it now, I knew that was the moment I'd decided that no monster, no villain, no tragedy—nothing would ever separate us again.

But he doesn't know, I reminded myself, *that I want things to change.*

We'd grown so close; close enough to share a horse, share a tent, share a *bed*. But to ask to share something more; to lay bare my emotions, open and unguarded; to risk making things awkward between us...

My heart seized at the thought. No, I couldn't tell him. What if it ruined everything we had?

What if it didn't?

I shook my head. Surely, if he'd dreamed of me as I'd dreamed of him, I'd know. If the devotion we carried for one another, the loyalty, the friendship, the respect, had ever grown into something more for him, I'd *know*. I wasn't blind anymore, if I had ever been; I could see my own mess of emotions like they were real, palpable things fluttering in my hands. And if he'd fallen half as much in love with me as I had with him—

I'd *know*.

So the answer was simple: I was alone in this. And that would just have to be all right.

I exhaled, leaning back against our borrowed bedroom door. There was little else to do in the stillness; I was dressed now, donning my day-old bloody armour with Bren's personal crest across my chest. But seeing it now, in my current mood, made me feel as I rarely did, and my hands shook.

He'd had it embroidered for me, years ago, on a stretch of dark brown leather in gold thread—seven trees, standing in a row of three, then four, with a rising sun cresting above the leaves. He'd had the emblem designed when he'd first become a knight, the symbol as recognizable as that of his father's or the Queen's. It was the only thing he'd kept from that part of his life.

You should wear it, instead of the King's, he'd said, when he'd handed it to me, *so you can carve your own legacy, away from his. With me.*

Touching it, knowing what it meant, my fingers running over the grooves in the thread, I felt warm—almost hot—as if possessed. I willingly carried his mark, and despite my inner conflict, I knew exactly what more I wanted from him. From *us*. What I *craved*.

And if I couldn't tell him, couldn't have him, then maybe...

I swallowed. With my eyes closed, I slid my hand over my hip, in search of a buckle I knew wasn't there. I'd already loosened it, pulling the metal from the tongue, leaving it to dangle against my leg.

Only a fool would waste this time, I thought. But whether I meant the time I'd lose was foolish—or failing to seize it was foolish—I didn't know or couldn't admit.

I pushed down my trousers, just enough to feel the bite of the cold, empty air on my skin. I shivered, not from the chill, but from some delayed sense of pure relief. My body had been pleading with me for *days*.

I filled my hand, trembling from the pressure, the first stroke so delicate I nearly shouted in half-agony, half-hope. I was wound as tight as a ball of string, and with the slightest pull, I began to unravel.

Idiot. Only an idiot would—

I swore. Slowly, roughly, I gave in, my body shaking as I stroked myself, my mind leaping to all the things I'd been imagining since the previous morning. Bren's legs, heavy against mine, his lips breathing me in. His hands in my hair, my wrists bound above me, the curves of his shoulders swallowing the sky. There was nothing to see; just him. Just us.

I'd never wanted anyone like this before; never ached for it, my body outside my control. But I did now, arching backwards in the darkness, a single sound caught high in my throat.

I nearly said his name; nearly moaned it, crying out. But I fought down the urge, exhaling quickly, quietly, letting my attention lapse for a single, blinding, glorious moment.

Then it was done, the pleasure carving through me like an arrow. All the tension, all the neediness, slipped from my body and stained my hand.

Gods above, I thought, through the haze. *I'm in trouble.*

CHAPTER SIX

Having to focus on doing my job—on hunting, on tracking, on following the faint sound of leathery wingbeats as they split open the sky—meant pretending, at least for now, that I could keep my eyes off of Bren. Off the sense of violence in his expression; off the determination that pounded his heels into the dirt. He was a beast in his own right, biting at the bars of his cage, desperate to sink his teeth into the enemy bearing down on us. But whether that enemy was the monsters we hunted, or his father's misplaced sense of pride, was impossible to say.

For my own small part in this, I just tried to keep my head on straight. I was supposed to be leading us, chasing *them*, gaining ground, but I could hardly manage it.

Instead, I was utterly and completely *distracted*, reimagining my own pleasure like I could still taste the tang of it in the air. And to be so *desperate*? So *eager*? It was all still a shock.

Then I started missing things, bigger and bigger things. Claw marks on dying trees, drag marks in disturbed soil, until at last I walked right past a body, mangled and bloody, less than three feet off the path. I hadn't seen it; *couldn't* see it. I was too preoccupied trying to figure out what to do about Bren.

"Are you all right?" he asked me. Once, twice. Maybe a third time? And despite hearing the worry in his voice, I waved it away.

Finally, after about an hour of this, Bren snapped out his hand and caught my wrist, moving so fast that it was only instinct that kept me from breaking my arm in his unrelenting grip. I staggered, jerking forward on the uneven forest floor, but twisted on my heel to face him, just in time to see him turn my palm towards the sky.

He wasn't being rough with me, exactly, but I could see from his tense, almost angry expression that he wanted to prove a point, and whatever he'd thought about my hand, he'd been right to think it. The harsh glimmer in his eyes told me so.

"Your heart's racing," he said, and I was so startled I almost missed it. In fact, my heart rate was so erratic, so frantic, it was making both my hands shake, and that was all the more apparent against Bren's steady, unwavering grip. I stared at him, and for a moment, my vision went entirely white.

Get a hold of yourself, I thought bitterly, but even shutting my eyes did little to stem the flurry of feeling that burst from my chest. It felt bright, and hot, and distinctly, overwhelmingly *dangerous*. Like I was about to say something I should absolutely, definitely *not*, under any circumstance, breathe into being.

"You're not upset with me, are you?" Bren asked, his tone suddenly gentle. The admission shot my eyes wide open, but drinking him in only rocked my emotions further, anchoring them to the glory of his open arms and open expression. He hadn't let me go, and I hadn't tried to pull away, but there was no mistaking my fluttering pulse lying bare in the otherwise empty space between us. "About the letter? About my father?"

I paled, staring at the side of his face, waiting for him to break out into a huge grin, laughing at himself—and at me—for genuinely believing he was uneasy about this, even for a moment. But Bren never broke character. He remained with his eyes facing forward, mouth set, jaw locked. If not for the quiet, I would've missed the moment he shifted his feet, the movement so slight that only the faint crinkle of the leaves under his boots gave him away.

"Of course not," I replied, and willed my hand to stop shaking. It worked, but only with tremendous effort. It was hard to feel the warmth of him, humming, electric, around the nerves in my wrist, so close to where my magic and my markings were etched against my skin. "You've kept your father off my back for years, and I've never regretted deserting. Or leaving the army. Or choosing you. And I never will."

I'd said too much, but at that, Bren only sighed, the sound rushing out of him all at once. He seemed to calm, to relax, his tense expression easing around his nose and his mouth, but he still hadn't released my hand. If anything, he held me tighter now, to the point the bones in my palm were starting to ache.

"You have to let go, Bren," I murmured, and the moment he realized what he was doing he dropped my hand.

"Ah," he said, and the word was hardly a word at all. I lowered my arm, flexing my fingers reflexively before forcing myself to stop.

There was a pause, heavy and awkward. Then, before I

met Bren's eyes again, I told myself I would see nothing but my best friend standing there when I raised my head, valiant but flawed, arrogant but kind, beautiful but only in a distant way, like anyone might think of a hero in a story-book. Instead, I found my decidedly soft-spoken, boyishly charming, unfairly attractive monster hunting partner of six years standing before me, with the most wounded expression I had ever seen on his face. It made me want to kiss him all the more, if that was possible.

"I'm sorry," we both said at once, into the stillness. His voice was louder than mine, bolder, more final, so I let my apology drift away with the wind.

"It's nothing," I added, and for good measure, patted him on the shoulder. The metal of his pauldron, dented and stained, engraved with his personal crest, felt cold against my hand, just like I ought to be. Reliable and protective, but separate, unaffected. I steeled myself and stepped away from him.

"If we hurry, we might still catch up to them," I said. Everything I could see was on the ground now: the roots, the dirt, the blood, the bones. I was too afraid to look up and betray myself—or my feelings—any further. "There's still daylight for a few hours yet. We should take the horse."

Behind me, Bren grunted in reply, but after a long moment, I heard him turn to follow. Whatever this was, whatever we were, I'd have to ignore it.

But as Bren climbed onto the saddle behind me, his body settling against every curve of my back and my legs, I found myself torn between melting into his touch or completely burning away.

$\approx$

In the end, it was the smell of blood that helped clear my head; the smell of bodies, dead or dying, that helped settle my nerves and pulled my thoughts from the warmth of Bren's hands. Before I'd met him, these hunts—long days spent tracking and chasing monsters three or four times my size—had been what I'd lived for, what I'd been *made* for. And it was no different now, even with Bren's arms wrapped tight around my waist, his breath hot in my hair. If I took a wrong turn, or misjudged an enemy, someone would die, and that would always be true.

"We're running out of road," I said suddenly, as the gaps in the fog and the trees up ahead opened wide to show nothing but the boundless, endless dark between us and the next day's dawn. "And the signs of a nest are everywhere."

But Bren wasn't really listening to me anymore, and behind me, I could feel his attention drift as his body twisted against the curve of the saddle. His tight hold around my waist began to loosen, and though I reached for his hands, to steady him, he only squeezed mine back. For a long moment, he didn't speak.

"What is it?" I asked, but then I turned my head before he could answer, following his gaze to the stretch of road behind us. My eyes adjusted, perhaps a second too slow, and saw only what I expected to see: a mile of winding dirt and translucent fog, thick and dark, pockmarked by green shadows that waved in the wind, the branches above our heads reaching down to cage us in.

Seeing my attention falter, my pull on the reins shifting our course to the right, Bren clicked his tongue, nudging my cheek with his hand so I faced forward again.

"Don't," he said, his voice low and urgent. At my hip, his fingers reached down to pull at my belt loops, as if hoping that would keep me in place. Instead, I jumped at the touch, burned by the heat of his hands and the graze of his thumb against my skin.

As we rounded another bend, gaining speed as we passed between two fallen trees, Bren leaned in, his mouth by my ear. "Don't look up," he said pointedly. "Don't look back. Just keep your eyes on the road and trust me with this."

"You have a plan?" I asked, throwing the words over my shoulder, the quiet sound of wingbeats sneaking through the trees again, so distant they were hardly anything at all. But I could place them now, closer than they'd ever been—and they were *behind* us.

"We've passed them?" I said, and still, he didn't answer. I wasn't sure what he could see, what he expected, but from the hush of his breath and the wail of the wind, I could guess. So I took him at his word and pressed our horse harder, made her run faster—and waited. For something. For anything at all to change in an instant.

We rode like this for what seemed like hours, the road disappearing beneath our horse's hooves as the gathering dark threatened to swallow us. The reaching trees and the gaping shadows hardly shifted, but as I chanced one look up, beyond the branches, beyond the fog, I caught sight of the sun as it slowly slipped across the sky, the horizon reaching out and through us as it stole back the afternoon light.

I said his name, then, urgent in a way I hadn't felt before. *What are you waiting for? The mists are coming.* But Bren only murmured the first part of my name back to me, seemingly unbothered, unconcerned, for all that he looked back frequently, twisting in the saddle.

"Keys," he said. "Trust me."

What else could I say? "I do," I told him. "I just know you're about to do something rash."

At that, Bren laughed, the sound shivering into my hair, rocking against my back, filling every empty inch of the space where our bodies met. "I'll try not to," he promised.

Hold steady was what he truly seemed to say, but he breathed no word of it. I reached for one of my swords, reacting to the shift in his body, the rising tension, but he pushed my hand away, his own sword staying buried in its sheath.

So again, I waited, trusting that he would signal when he meant to, act when it was time. I leaned forward on our horse, pressing for more speed, but as her breath began to labour and her legs began to slow, I knew we were running out of time.

"Bren," I said, but he shushed me with a squeeze, his hand on my thigh.

At last, I heard the shrill sound of piercing cries fill the space all around us, until it seemed like every bird in the world was falling out of the sky.

"They're diving," Bren said, so quietly I almost missed it beneath the howling. His mouth was right by my ear, so close I felt the ghost of his lips on my skin. "There has to be a dozen. Maybe more. Clawed feet, with sharp teeth. Wings. Bloody mouths."

It was a pity monsters came with no names. "Can we outrun them?" I asked, eyes still ahead. It was taking everything in me not to cover my ears and pitch us from the saddle, our bodies shielded on one side by the dirt. Anything to protect us—to protect *him*.

Bren let go of my waist. "Not anymore," he said. "Stay behind me."

And with that, I turned only in time to watch him

dismount backwards over the saddle, landing hard on his feet before twisting towards the descending horde of enemies. His armour clanged together as he moved, loud against the din, and as he drew his sword, he struck the hilt against his breastplate, filling the road with sound like a battering ram.

A heartbeat later, I launched myself after him, hitting the ground a few feet from his shadow. But even then, reacting within an instant of his last word, the attack had already begun.

Ringed by leaves and splintered branches, the monsters thundered onto the road, their massive, bloody wings only wretched, horrid things held together by feathers and blackened skin. They all missed Bren, twisting on the ground like misfired arrows, but their bodies recoiled as if made purely from bone, their movements stiff and jerky. Then they howled, screeching like dying cats, their eyes a milky, inhuman white, their mouths opening wide enough to bite through his chest.

Unflinching, Bren swung his sword in long, sweeping strokes, cutting through wings and scaled, bird-like feet to the sound of high-pitched cries ripped from their throats. One creature, easily twice his height, lunged blindly at his massive blade, only for Bren to cut straight through it, bursting what remained of its mutated body and spraying its blackened blood into the dirt. Another beast, wiser than the first, leapt toward the sky and slashed at Bren from above, its long legs and piercing claws tearing at his skin.

In the chaos, the best I could do was avoid the wide swing of Bren's blade, then come up behind him and slash at the creatures as they focused their attention on all the noise he was making. Because there, at the center of the madness, his yells and hollers kept their attention, his armour deflecting their claws and teeth with loud bangs that seemed to drive them mad.

And Bren was unrelenting, always moving, hardly dodging, striking high. But he was bleeding too; I could see the splash of redness dirtying his face, their monstrous hands cutting in from every angle, their clawed feet reaching for his shoulders as if trying to carry him away.

I couldn't heal him, not without distracting him, but from behind him, I stabbed another creature down to the hilt, its body twisting around my blade, ripping its arm and part of its shoulder from its body as it pulled itself away. But the momentum created an opening, and the beast tore into Bren's back, its teeth biting at his neck with its mouth of bloody, black gums, its long legs fumbling around him as it tried to lift off into the air.

Instinctually, I dropped my swords, then grabbed its wings with both my hands and ripped it from Bren with strength that didn't belong to me. I felt fear, hot and wild in my throat, and worse—I felt angry. Brazen. Reckless. I timed a pulse of magic with my breath, flaring a bright burst of power down all of my fingers and into the creature's bleeding shoulders, where I lunged for the gaping hole left by the arm I'd torn off its body.

At once, a vicious, golden light tore from the gash, ripping the creature's back wide open and carving through all the bones in its chest. Anything I had slashed or cut split apart like torn paper, the rest of its body crumpling onto the road like a wet rag.

It made me feel powerful, almost god-like—enough that I killed another, and then a third, while that golden light still poured from my hands. The next nearest creature reared back at the brush of my fingers, roaring on its flailing legs with its arms spread wide, only to splinter like cracked wood.

They couldn't have stopped me—nothing in the entirety of the woods could've stopped me. But as I turned, glancing around at the mess between the trees, at the quarter mile of road that was bathed in black and red, at the fleshy mounds of skin and feathers gathering in the wheel wells left behind by long forgotten carts, I found the rest of the screeching, screaming mass had died at the end of Bren's sword, his every stroke barrelling through them, beheading some, pulverizing others.

Even as the last lay dead at his feet, Bren reared back and pulled his blade straight through a twitching body, shearing the monster's right wing and destroying what was left of its chest. Beside it, a pile of blood and limbs roiled in the heat from the battle, finally growing silent and still.

"Let's hope that's the worst of it," Bren said, speaking first into the quiet, wiping his mouth with the back of his hand and smearing more black ooze across his chin and his cheeks. He was horrifically bloody, from his jawline to his ankles, but stood with his head held high, seemingly quite satisfied. Then he regarded me, my wrists still alight with magic, the bright flare of power burning away in my chest. And he smiled. "Do you think there's a river nearby?"

I dropped my gaze, let my power slip away, and bent down to sheathe both of my blades. I wasn't sure, but the gods knew to what lengths I'd go to find out. "Let's look."

CHAPTER SEVEN

The adrenaline that had carried me through the fight wore away as I loosened the laces on Bren's boots. In my chest, an emptiness yawned where my magic had been, the sense of loss as material as stone. I was tired, and I carried that openly in how I moved: in my slouched shoulders, my heavy eyelids, my aching head. But to put words to the complaint would've been a disservice to Bren, who was covered head to toe in red and black bruises.

Every piece of his armour he removed only revealed more injuries. His elbows were swollen, as was one of his knees, and his neck had been torn raw by two sets of teeth. The outsides of his thighs were dotted with gashes, his back horribly slashed, and his shoulders were so tender he needed my help removing his breastplate to avoid spilling more of his blood.

As we worked, we didn't speak, and in short order Bren was sitting in the grass in only his underclothes, his body battered, bloody, and beaten. He stretched in the shade of a massive oak tree, his feet dipping down into the shallow pond we'd found by the road. The bite of the water and the chill of the wind seemed to soothe his blistered ankles.

"That was hard," he said at last, twisting his body this way and that, testing to see where it hurt the most, how much mobility he had. "But you're all right?"

I looked up from where I'd sat down beside him, my chin resting on my upraised knees. I had hardly been touched in the chaos, just jostled around, clipped by a wingtip or the sharp side of a claw. But knowing his plan now, that he'd always intended to keep their attention on himself—that even in the sky, fifty feet away, he'd seen their milky white eyes and guessed they'd hunted mostly by ear— I tried to see the bravery of it. The brilliance. After all, they were dead, and we were not.

But things were rarely that simple.

"I'm entirely unhurt," I said, lowering my feet into the pond next to his, trying not to touch him—and hurt him—in the process. But with the movement, the colour of the water deepened from a ruddy blue to a bloody black, the silt at the bottom mixing with the torn scabs on both of his legs. "You should've told me what you'd planned."

Instead of answering, Bren raised one corner of his mouth, his right eyebrow arching to match. "I'm fine, Keenyn," he said softly. "Don't look at me like that. The bruises will heal; you know they will."

In response, I gestured broadly at his body, at the discolouration marring his skin. Then past him, at the forest of dangers just waiting to swallow him. "I'm saying I could've *helped* you. You look like you've been run over by a horse, then two more besides. It pains me to see you like this."

"Does it?" Bren replied, something serious creeping into the edge of his voice. His brow furrowed, and though the bruise on his jaw was turning yellow before my eyes, I knew the worst of it was still to come. "I never would've guessed. Your concern for me hasn't shown in your face at all."

I blinked, my mouth falling half-open in obvious protest. But then Bren *smiled*, his expression becoming so warm, so affectionate, that I could hardly stand it.

He's teasing me, I realized too late, staring at the mirth on his face as if it could distract me from my own utter shock.

"Seven gods, Bren," I said, holding out my hands, though it was only by some unseen grace that they weren't shaking. "You have to let me heal you. You're trying to cheer me up—you must have lost a lot of blood."

At that, Bren shook his head, then closed his eyes and leaned back on his hands. Above us, the failing sunlight rippled across his body like shadows and stars, the warmth drowning in the thick layer of leaves that blocked the sky.

When he finally turned back to me, his eyes the colour of a storm, he said, "Can I ask you something?"

"Of course," I replied.

"I can feel you, when you use your magic," he said, though his eyes looked past me now, beyond the water, beyond the nearby trees. "Your body. Your heartbeat. Is it like that with everyone you heal?"

I swallowed, thinking back on our last afternoon in the woods, with the recruits; on the hunger that came from holding him, intimately, under my hands. The thought stirred something ravenous inside of me.

"It's less, with strangers," I admitted into the quiet. "The magic carries an awareness between us, as it would with anyone, but the more it's done, the more it..." I hesitated, searching for the words. "The more the magic *recognizes* you, I suppose. Recognizes what it would mean if you were whole. It wants to fix, to mend, to purify, as if you were just an extension of me. It's a deeper connection if the contact is repeated."

As he listened, Bren leaned closer to me, so close I could count the freckles around his nose. I had to look away— away from his eyes, from the curves of his lips; from his jaw, sharp and defined, like etchings in marble. But as I glanced up at his hair, all I saw was more blood.

"But why can I sense you?" he asked, his voice low. "I can't heal you back."

At that, I could only shrug. "The awareness is the cost of the closeness," I said. "It binds us, opening us both to the reach of the magic. Through touch, you *become* me, in a way. So you know all my aches and pains as if they were your own. It's how I know all of yours, as well."

Realizing, then, that his questions were just meant to stall me, to delay the healing, I held out my hands again. Higher. Closer to his face. "I know it's a strange feeling," I said, my palms just brushing his cheeks, "but if you concentrate on yourself, on your wounds as they heal, you won't sense me as much. The sensations will pass, and you'll be able to continue riding today."

Bren paused, letting my fingers tangle in a few loose curls of his hair. I thought, perhaps, that he might kiss my hand again, or shy away, but he didn't move.

After a moment, I finally felt him relax. Give in. "Mm," was all he said, but I knew.

Gingerly, then, I cradled his face between my hands, feeling the cringe in his jaw as he braced against the discomfort. Even from this, from the lightest touch under his chin, the degree to which he'd been bludgeoned by those beasts was more apparent, more severe. He'd clearly been hiding a lot of pain from me.

But he didn't speak; didn't give voice to it, didn't ask me to stop. So I held him, steady and sure, and flared the magic deep within me, the bright light enveloping all the markings on my arms before I let it spread out and consume him.

Immediately, I felt what little reserve I had left wasting away, all the energy and effort I still had in my body moving directly from me to him.

I couldn't heal everything; such a surge of healing magic, desperate and wild, would surely kill me. But I could do something, here and there, stitching his skin back together, easing his pain, helping him breathe.

I worked slowly, reaching down, deep, across his arms and through his body. I healed the bite marks on his neck, the sores on his ankles, the nasty welt on his thigh. I healed the gash on his head, lifted the black from his eyes, soothed the strain in his back.

But the weakness came for me quickly, and with a start, I pulled away. For a moment, I couldn't see. My head throbbed, and my chest ached.

Seeing me sway, Bren caught my hand, then quickly grabbed my waist, keeping me upright. I groaned, low in my throat. I'd overdone it.

We were quiet for a long time, him and I, unmoving as my vision slowly came back to me. Around us, the forest and the undergrowth, once luscious and green, turned foul and dark. All the while, the wind howled louder, pressing ever closer. We'd have to ride hard to outpace the mists tonight.

"We should go," I finally murmured, my lips slow to form the words. Even my tongue felt sluggish, like I'd taken energy from absolutely everywhere. "You should let go."

But he didn't; not right away. Instead, Bren stayed quiet, as if waiting for my breathing to steady, my migraine to pass.

"You're an idiot," he said at last, his voice too loud, his mouth too close to mine. "What good is healing me if it kills you?"

I hiccupped. It hurt everywhere, right down to my bones. "I'm fine," I said, lying with as much of a straight face as I could muster. "I can walk."

And with that, Bren let me pull away, but watched as I dragged myself to my feet. I avoided his eyes, stumbling back to our horse, only to untie the reins and realize I wasn't wearing boots.

Dimly, I heard Bren walk up behind me and touch my arm. He was gentle, but his tone was insistent. "You can't focus—" he started to say.

But I raised both my hands, as if to keep my consciousness from slipping away, and Bren fell silent again.

"I need to sit," I said, but the words were slurred now, and I took only half a breath. Then I stumbled, felt my legs lock up. The world spun.

And instead of kneeling, I crumpled in his arms, my muscles refusing to hold me.

CHAPTER EIGHT

In the long hour that followed, lost to the tangle of the fog, I sat quietly in Bren's lap, my head against his shoulder and my legs over his knee. Behind me, his one arm held me steady, as it had when he'd carried me here; and at my hip, his other hand held his sword, unsheathed and menacing, in front of his legs. A monstrous thing, the tip of his blade was as wide as his hand, and it gouged into the dirt by my foot like a fence post, boxing us in. If I shifted my gaze, I could just catch a glimpse of our reflection in the metal, his bare chest, arms, and legs like a taunt next to mine, his armour and boots still by the pond.

I couldn't move, and for a while, I could hardly see—but as colour came back to me, then sound, I became acutely aware of how faintly Bren was breathing, and each time I shuddered, gasping, he held his breath, waiting for me to steady.

"Are you warm enough?" Bren finally asked, a few hours into his vigil. I couldn't nod, despite wanting to, but with half a shrug, Bren eased his heavy wool cloak from his pile of discarded clothes and draped it over me, assuming the answer. "Don't you dare die. I'm not going anywhere."

And he didn't; he stayed exactly where he was, almost perfectly still, his back against a fallen tree, his body heat keeping me alive. It was all he understood, about the cost of the magic; that overusing it made me tired, and kept my hands cold. But I'd rarely drawn this much before—and I'd never collapsed in front of him. It explained how anxious he was, how paranoid, and how gently he held my body against his chest.

It took another few hours before I could speak, and more still to find the courage, but by then, the words I'd wanted to say had changed a thousand times. There was simply no avoiding the truth—I'd made an emotional decision. A stupid one. Bren had seen it on my face.

"I'm sorry," I finally whispered, as the quiet that came with nightfall broke through the trees. "I was just trying to help."

Startled, Bren nodded, the knuckles of his right hand—gripping his sword hilt—turning white. "Let that be a lesson, then," he said softly, after a moment's hesitation, "but don't try to talk. Just rest. I've got you."

Instead, with what little strength I had, I moved my hand up to loosen where my armour was pulling against my throat. At once, Bren's hand met mine, sensing the effort and trapping my palm, the leather tearing in his hand.

"I was just—" he started to say, but stopped when he realized he'd torn open my shirt, my collarbone lying bare beneath his hand. I didn't respond; just listened to his voice, scratchy and raw, as he fumbled for something else to fill the silence. "You...shouldn't try to move."

Faintly, I was aware of him turning his head again, the movement bringing our lips too close together. One shift, and he'd be kissing me instead, our legs tangling on top of each other's in the grass.

It was impossible not to think about, especially when he ran his fingers through my hair, easing my head higher on his shoulder, the corner of my mouth brushing his skin. At my throat, our hands were still together, my pulse slow and faint beneath his thumb. If I raised my chin, inching closer, and he—

No. I blinked and forced myself to look away, afraid to let those feelings, that *urgency*, get the better of me. Even here, even now, as I veered on the edge of unconsciousness, I was *weak.*

"You've never been so careless before," Bren said suddenly, breathing the words out against me. Maybe that was all he wanted; all he'd wanted to say. "You're better than this. I know you are."

I swallowed against the weight of my tongue, my mouth dry, my lungs aching. "I made a mistake," I managed to whisper, and though my voice broke from the strain, I cleared my throat and carried on. "I overreached. I was worried about you."

"I was fine," Bren said, and his expression held nothing gentle for me, nothing kind. "So I don't know what you were thinking. After everything we've been talking about, everything we've survived, did you even wonder what would've happened to me, if this had killed you? Did you think that through at all?"

I hadn't, and the truth of that burned on the way down. "You would've made it," I said, murmuring the words against his shoulder. "To Warrenhall. Before the mists came."

There was a long pause after that, heavy and drawn out, before Bren made a sound at the back of his throat. "You'd still be dead," he said, and I heard the anger in his voice now, creeping in. "And I'd have half a life without you."

That sentiment settled, unexpected and warm, in the curves of my cheeks, brightening them with colour. He had no idea what he was doing to me, whispering like that, while his bare chest hummed against me as he spoke. "We're a team," I replied, my voice husky. "You didn't have to see how bloody and awful your injuries were. If we'd just fought those winged creatures together from the start—"

"Keenyn," Bren said, "I don't need your permission to protect you. They could've killed you. It was less of a risk to keep their attention on just me."

I closed my eyes, pulling my gaze from the twist of his mouth and the wall of living shadow, endless and horrid, rising up to drown us. "And what if they'd killed you instead? What then?" I said, bewildered that we were arguing the same thing, in different words. "You're my whole world, Bren. It's also my job to protect *you*. You just have to get your big head out of the way sometimes."

That first admission snuck past me before I could stop it. Gods above, my face felt hot.

"Bren, please," I said, taking the easy way out, desperate to break the silence that had rushed in between us. "It's getting late, and the mists are coming. We should set up the tent—it's all we have. I can help you."

He eyed me, and the matter of who was to blame, of missteps, of mistakes, lay buried like the tip of his sword. And like before, it was clear there was still more to say, even if neither of us was prepared to say it.

"Let me carry you, then," he said, tightening his grip on my waist, "so we can stay together." His ears had turned red, and the anger on his tongue had cooled to something...

soft. "Don't fight it—don't argue. You can't walk. Just let me work."

And though I nodded, finding the strength, I purposefully avoided meeting his gaze.

When Bren and I had first met, on a cold and dark summer morning, he'd been all of twenty, and I'd been a week shy of twenty-one. He'd been cockier then, reckless in a way that was hard to recognize now, and never wore armour that wasn't plated with gold. Looking back, he could've been anything, done anything, and been with anyone, but the weight of a whispered prophecy had long since rubbed him raw, and after I'd saved his life on that first night we'd served together, he never thought of the frontier wars in the same way again. Carving through the forest, setting up outposts; the cost of life was too high, and he'd seen that firsthand. The forest fought back—viciously, ruthlessly. He'd settle for a single partner and less glamorous guild work instead.

That was the secret he'd told me when no one else was listening, when we'd laid together beneath the trees on a night it had rained and thundered, when we'd listened to the violence of the storm rattling off the canvas tarp he'd pitched above our heads.

Move closer to me, he'd said, afterwards, *so you don't get wet.* We'd even shared a pillow he'd stolen from his father's tent, his head resting gently against mine. Back then, the closeness had come from knowing him, befriending him; from having nowhere else either of us wanted to be. I may have outranked him in name and title, but when I was with him, I wasn't a prince fourth in line for the throne, risking my life in the vanguard of the Queen's army—I was his mage, his healer, his rearguard, his shield, and to everyone else in camp, he was simply *mine*.

Six years later, and in many ways, I'd grown to be his equal. I was more than his insurance, his safety net, his friend; I was *his*. We could spar without fear, trust without question. Between us, the only boundaries were secrets, personal and dark.

And whether we'd meant for it to happen or not, I'd come to know him. He'd come to know me.

It was how I knew, in the dead of night, that he wanted to talk. That after everything we'd been through, everything that had brought us to this point, there was something weighing on him, something that needed to be said, even as he woke me, exhausted, unwilling.

"I would stay up, if I could," he said, the mists swirling in around his hands, filling the tent. He'd been sitting in the mouth of the canvas keeping watch, his hips against my legs, his eyes locked on the forest beyond, forever hunting for something half-alive. "But I can hardly keep my eyes open."

I sat up, as he spoke, and swapped places with him, our faces passing so closely that I could've counted the freckles dusting his nose. "You should've woken me sooner," I replied, letting my shoulders fill the opening he'd left behind, my boots in the grass, my back to the mists. It was a wonder we both fit in the space with Bren still in his armour, ready to fight. "We could've done four shifts, if you were tired."

Wearily, Bren's gaze drifted from the ceiling of the tent to my hands, drinking me in. Then, abruptly, he leaned forward, bringing shadows across his face to cover his eyes.

In the darkness, I thought his expression seemed pained. Upset. Angry. "Can I do nothing right by you?" he whispered. "Am I always doing something wrong?"

Reflexively, I touched him. Touched his cheek, his jaw, the very edge of his mouth. "That's not what I'm saying," I replied, overwhelmed by my own reaction, by how normal it was. Worse, I had nowhere to go, not without stepping outside—and in here, in the blackness, there was only Bren and his burning hands and his reddening face. I pulled my fingers away. "I just—"

But Bren had turned away as I spoke, moving so suddenly that it caught me off guard. "You should go," he said, holding up his hand. "I'm going to say something I regret."

His voice was hard now, almost icy. Restrained. But in that moment, I could see right through him.

"Talk to me," I said, shifting my body deeper into the darkness. Behind me, the canvas flap fell completely closed, sealing us into the tent.

In the quiet, cut off from the world, our voices were muffled only by the sound of our breathing. "Something's bothering you."

Bren's eyes met mine, our faces still so close that despite the darkness, I could've traced every line on his swollen lips. He'd been biting them, teasing them between his teeth, the force enough to draw blood to the surface. "Someone has to be out there," he said, deflecting. "Keeping watch. Standing guard."

I turned at his request, making a show of lifting the tent flap and looking around, scanning the night and the trees for the shadows and eyes of something evil, something dead. Then I set it back down, blocking out the mists. "Your thoughts, Bren," I said, tapping on his knee like a drum. "Out with it."

"I swear to the gods, you drive me mad."

"Fascinating. But that's not news."

"There's nothing to say."

I waited, letting the tension fill the tent almost to bursting. "It's something, Bren," I said, and in my chest, I felt dread turn my lungs into stone. "You can tell me."

Finally, he said, "You're the one who's not talking to me!"

"About what?"

"I don't know!"

It was a standstill, our words pointless. Silly.

We both sighed at the same time.

"For the love of the gods," Bren said. "You've been looking at me differently for days. I can't stand it. Just tell me what it is, if there's some stupid thing I've said or done, so I can apologize and clear the air between us. Please."

My entire stomach dropped, filling my ribs with a sense of nothingness. Endlessness. Every inch of my chest felt hollow.

"I—"

My face flushed, and I let the sound die out on my tongue, then tried again.

"It's nothing you've done," I said, but I said it too quickly. Too loudly.

How could I tell him? How could I destroy us?

"It's nothing. I promise it's nothing."

Bren's expression was flat. "The gods know why I try," he mumbled, rubbing his temples. And with that, he fell back against the ground and closed his eyes.

"Sort yourself out, Keenyn," he said. "It's going to get one of us killed if you don't."

CHAPTER NINE

It struck me, in the long grass just outside the tent, wrapped in the silence of the mists, that I should've just kissed Bren. That I should've leaned in, pulled him close, and pressed his mouth to mine, silencing those burning questions and swallowing them off his tongue. Maybe then, I'd have an answer—good or bad, at least I'd *know*—and I wouldn't have had to sit out here for hours, with this dull ache between my legs, wondering what might've, could've, should've been.

Now, I wasn't sure what to do or how to fix this; how to apologize. So I just closed my eyes, ran my fingers through my hair, and tried to put it behind me. Patching things up with Bren would be a problem for the morning, when the world was lush and green again, and when the tremble in my hands was the last thing that gave me away.

But it was then, in the quiet halfway to dawn, that I heard a twig *snap*.

I was on my feet in a heartbeat, drawing one of my blades. I held the hilt loosely, with the metal angled towards the grass, as I scanned the darkness for glowing eyes, wild and angry. But nothing seemed to move, in the stillness, until I felt a tug.

It happened in an instant. Whatever was behind me wrenched my sword from my hand, sweeping it out from under me. I was pulled with the movement, jerking nose-first into the ground, but rolled, drawing my other sword in the process.

"Bren!" I yelled, my attention behind the tent. Because there, in the gloom, I saw a figure wrapped in broken moonlight.

Whoever—whatever—it was, it looked like me.

Holding my sword, the silhouette slipped from the shadows and the mists like a reflection from a mirror, its skin the same light grey as my own, its hair black, its eyes dark. It had even donned a perfect replica of my armour, down to Bren's personal crest on my chest. The only difference at all was at its throat, where a long, vicious tongue slipped from a second mouth, licking my double's face. It had no second set of teeth or lips; just this, just this tongue, forked and red and horrid.

In that same moment, Bren dove from the tent across our camp, putting as much space between him and his temporary bed as one burst of movement would allow. He had no context, no information, but he was ready; his eyes blazed, his head turning rapidly until he found me, his hand gripping both his sword and its sheath, the leather straps loose from their bindings.

"Keenyn?"

"*Bren.*"

Whipping around, Bren's attention shot to my double, to the sword in its hand—no, in its *leg*. There was no second tongue now, just blood splattered across its body.

"*It's a copy!*" it yelled, its voice—*my* voice—now strangled with pain. My sword had pierced all the way through its thigh, its hands shaking in terror. *"There's a tongue in its throat! Rip it out!"*

Stunned, I watched as Bren made a decision. The *wrong* decision. And in a flurry, barrelled right toward me.

Gods, no.

I raised my second blade to parry him, hating the thought of hurting him, but the force of the strike nearly broke all the bones in my hand. *He might actually kill me*, I realized, a menacing coolness coming over his face. He'd never hit me this hard before, with all his strength; he'd never meant to.

"Wait!" I yelled, knowing I sounded just like that thing, that creature. "Don't listen to it!"

But Bren was already swinging again, his sword like a hurricane. He came down from overhead, moving through a fighting form I'd seen him practise a thousand times. There was no blocking this; the momentum alone would split my skull.

So I dodged out of the way, taking off into the trees, then circled back around the tent and tried dashing towards the monster. In the dirt, it thrashed uselessly at its self-imposed injury, my mirrored face twisting in agony, my echoed voice crying out in pain. Then, as it rolled across the grass, it drew the same dagger I always kept at my thigh into its own bloody hand, holding it in front of its face.

Instinctually, I reached for that same blade, but found it gone, the sheath empty. This creature had outsmarted me in every regard except one.

I had magic.

Bursting from the darkness, I tried to slash at the creature's face—but for once, Bren was faster than me. He hardly made a sound; just shielded the creature with the

69

entirety of his body, using his own gloved hand to catch the downward swing of my sword.

It was like hitting a tree. Bren was solid, unflinching. He threw me back, then swung his blade and tried to impale me again.

This time, I had nowhere to go, no ability to dodge. He caught me in the ribs, his sword slicing through my armour and tearing through my skin, scraping bone. I cried out in shock, feeling something splinter, something break.

I pulled back immediately, trying to heal. But as the golden light burst from around my wrists, shining down my forearms, I felt something else inside me *die*. And the creature, thinking quickly, yelled, *"It's a trick! It's stolen my magic!"*

Unbelievable.

With a lunge, I broke across the clearing, stepping completely through the walls of our tent. The canvas buckled, curling around my legs, the poles and ropes snapping outward, swinging wildly.

And in my body, the magic in my chest flared red hot like the sun, healing me by hurting me, taking the energy from everywhere—my heart, my lungs, my hands, my eyes— which had only just recovered.

I couldn't do that again—couldn't heal, couldn't destroy.

But again, without pause, Bren charged forward with all his strength, his blade striking from the widest, broadest angles, the reach of his arm well beyond mine.

He held nothing back. He slashed with a shallow plunge, nearly cleaving through my face, then swung high, a few strands of my hair splitting apart on the sharpness of his blade.

My mind was freezing up, in my panic. What else could

I do? What could I say? His rage was a distraction, his aim relentlessly close.

Then he cut through me, skinning my leg as I parried again and tried to roll away. My blood stained the dirt, throwing the smell of metal into the air.

And behind him, all I could see was that monster wearing my face, its twin mouths grinning wildly, twirling my dagger in its hand like this was just a bit of fun.

I couldn't reach it. Bren would never let me past him, never stop fighting to protect what he thought was the real me. I knew it from the glint of determination I saw in his eyes, which I'd always admired, always adored.

So I dropped my sword.

"Bren, it's me," I said, my hands out, my feet moving half a step backwards. "You *know* me. I taught you how to dance. How to sing."

He slowed at once, jerking to the side, his next sword swing missing me on purpose and slamming into the ground. "What?"

It all came rushing up—random things, specific things. I could drown him in a thousand truths about me, about him, about *us.*

But only one thing seemed to matter. "I love you."

It seemed to click. Mouth open, body slack, I'd drawn all of Bren's attention; but at his back, that creature now stood within stabbing range, and it had two of my blades.

I pushed past him, bleeding, aching, and he spun with me. I stepped so close that I could see the whites of his eyes.

Then the creature lunged, my bloody sword still in its leg, my dagger raised, both mouths wide open. It started screaming "*Bren! Bren!*" like a manic echo.

I let it try and stab me, its attack clipping the tip of my ear, before my one hand shot out to smother it, breaking its nose. Then, with the other, I pulled my bloody sword out of its leg and spun it, forcing the blade completely through its ribs and down to the hilt in its chest.

Whatever it was made of—flesh and bone, or rot and tree roots—it felt soft under my sword and collapsed immediately from the pain. In my own mirrored face, I saw fear, panic, and then death, the lifelessness a curse, showing me something I didn't want to see.

I let it fall, its body a dark bundle of limbs and tongues in the dirt, its last few tremors lost to the grass. My heart rate steadied, the hush of the night returned, but my left leg throbbed, and my chest felt hollow.

Numb, I turned back to Bren, feeling like an eternity had passed, expecting to see him smile. Instead, he was standing two feet behind me, his eyes on the body, his expression vacant. Then he glanced at me, the real me, and sighed. It was the smallest, saddest sound I'd ever heard him make.

"Forgive me," he whispered, and he pinched the bridge of his nose, breathing deeply. Even from here, I could see that he was shaking, and he'd left his sword buried three feet in the dirt. "I didn't know. I just had to react so fast—"

I stepped forward, grabbing his hands, and met his eyes. His lips were parted and cherry red, even in the blackness of the hour.

His expression changed immediately, from something apologetic to something urgent. "Keenyn, what you said—"

"Can I kiss you?" I breathed out, the words slipping from me all in a rush. I hadn't once moved my gaze from his mouth, and if he leaned any closer, it would tear me apart.

Bren closed his eyes, and for a moment, his body went rigid in my hands. "Say that again?" he whispered, sounding confused. "Please?"

All the strength left my body. "I'm sorry, I didn't—"

He kissed me.

Bren and his beautiful, glorious mouth, insistent and hot, closed the distance between us and kissed me.

Immediately, every part of our bodies slotted together. He was everything, everywhere, his hands wrapped tightly around my waist, our chests completely flush. His mouth moved over mine, careful and unsure, and I kissed him fiercely, threading my fingers through his hair, feeling him shudder. He made a small, muffled sound of surprise, then gave in, kissing me harder, laughing against my mouth in what I could only describe as pure joy.

"Please," he demanded, as he chased my lips ruthlessly, his mouth quick to swallow the sounds we made. "Gods, let me have this."

Then, in the next breath, he swore against my chin. "Damn it, Keenyn," he said, and broke the kiss to trail his lips down my jaw, burying his mouth against my throat, pressing his teeth against my skin. I groaned, powerless to stop that feeling, that *longing*, from tearing right through me. "Do you have any idea how long I've—"

He cut himself off, the twist of his mouth drawing my attention. And he was blushing now, his cheeks a vibrant red that transformed the lines of his face.

"Kiss me again," I urged him, and he leaned back towards me, the kiss deeper and rougher, his hair in my eyes, his fingers on my shoulders and the back of my neck. Then his hand dipped lower, into the collar of my shirt, and lower still, until he was just above where I needed him most.

I nearly bucked into his hand, enthralled by how bold he was, but held still, letting him tease me—until he pushed his tongue past my lips, into my mouth, and the horror of how aroused I was came out as a stutter.

"Bren," I said, and he immediately stopped, his expression going static, his eyes half-closed. "Seven gods, if you regret this, you have to tell me. If we push things and it's not what you want, I'll go *mad*."

And at that, Bren just smirked, wild and wolfish, before kissing me again like he'd drown if he stopped.

CHAPTER TEN

Somewhere between one touch and the next, when I found the moment, the time, to raise my head, taking him in, I finally saw Bren for all that he was—his face flushed, his eyes alight, and his lips kiss-swollen and tender. "I've been blind, haven't I?" I said, my voice shaking. "How long— How long have you wanted this?"

And Bren's first response, soft and endearing, was just to say, "Since the day I met you."

The words were as desperate as the push and pull of his body, his lips lost in my hair, his fingers where I wanted his mouth to be—behind me, against me, in the gaps between my clothes, his palms against my skin.

"That's a long time," I said, but he was quick to muffle the words by kissing me again, holding me in place.

"On all the gods, Keenyn," he said, "I swear I've dreamed of nothing but you in six years. Nothing and no one but you."

I shivered, hearing that, and his admission brought something to life in my chest that I'd never realized was there. Something bright, something safe; something that belonged—and had always belonged—solely to Bren.

I breathed in the essence of him, helpless and wild, as his hands roamed over the parts of my body that only he had ever seen. It was perfect; *he* was perfect. I just needed—

In the quiet, I pulled Bren in, as close as the space would allow, and kissed him harder, more roughly, until he backed me up against a tree.

"You've been holding back," I said, and he smirked, his voice low, his tone husky.

"What you've done to me, Keenyn," he said, "all these months, all these years. You've left me wanting, *aching*."

I cursed, pulling his lips back towards me, ablaze with it —with this *feeling*, this urgency, unrelenting, unrestrained— so confident in the sweep of my tongue against his that I was surprised when he twisted away, dodging the warmth of my hands.

But before I could say anything, apologize, Bren caught both my wrists in one hand and pulled them up, over my head, his mouth pressing firmly against my brow. His breath was hot, his grip tight and heavy, and he lingered there, shaking against me.

"You're a menace," he said, and he kissed me again, grinding our hips together until I groaned. "Absolutely insatiable."

"I *need* this," I said, breathing the words out against him. "And for the love of the gods, tell me how I *missed* this."

By my ear, Bren laughed with the softest, most ravenous sound, mouthing the truth against my body like he'd been imagining this moment as I had. "Every bath we've ever shared, every saddle. Every bed. You've always been there, pressed up against me. I've never hidden it from you."

"Never?" I said, but Bren was far from finished, his other hand searching and reckless now, pulling at the ties and straps on my armour.

"You have no sense of it," he murmured, his pulse jumping where I could see it, the movement fluttering at his throat. "How long I've hoped for this. How much I've always wanted you, here, beneath me, just like this."

He kissed me again and I moaned against his mouth, letting him angle my head up towards him just as the top half of my armour came apart in his hands.

"Tell me where you want me to be," he said, and he was grinning now, consumed by this in a way I'd never seen before. "Tell me what you want. Or tell me to stop. I'm yours, Keenyn. I always have been."

I decided, immediately, as I strained against his hands, trapped against this tree by his hips and his legs, that I loved this part of him too. Feral, demanding, and *weak*—for this, for *me*.

My next sharp intake of breath was a hiss across my teeth. "I want you to step back," I said, "and let me go."

Bren hesitated, then nodded, dropping my wrists, and between us, he created the tiniest possible gap, his chest heaving, his expression dark. Then his gaze lowered, following my hands as I reached for his belt.

"I've wanted this too," I said, my voice steady, unflinching. I felt brazen, with nothing but this glint of silver in my palm, the latch opening under my thumb. "So let me enjoy this. Enjoy *you*."

Bren drank me in, unable to look away, his bright blue eyes following me as I dropped to my knees at his feet.

Then he reached for my hair, pushing back the strands that had tangled in my lips, my mouth level with his hips, his breathing choked, his hands shaking.

"Take off your pants, Bren," I said.

And he did. Quickly, hastily, with the force of a man trying not to destroy all his clothes in the process. Then, with a shove, he was bare before me in a wide expanse of pale skin, his belt bunched loosely at his knees, utterly shameless. Trembling.

I leaned in, my lips parted and dark, my tongue getting the barest taste of him, my body needy and wholly, undeniably sure.

"Gods," Bren breathed out. "You're beautiful."

"Hold on to me," I said, and above me, Bren cursed, my mouth darting out to take that long, urgent part of him against my tongue, swallowing around the base of him, along the length of him. He shuddered, nearly crying out.

It was so much. *He* was so much. And all of this—every groan, every sigh, every sound I pulled from him, every twitch—took me closer, took me with him.

I inched forward as far as I dared, until he hit the back of my throat, and Bren nearly doubled over.

"Keenyn, *fuck*," he said, and he pulled my hair, anchoring us both as I pulled away, then did it all over again. "Seven gods—"

Above me, Bren made the deepest, most desperate sound, bucking against my hands, trying to control himself but failing, miserably, as he bit into his wrist. I let him guide me, direct me, but caught glimpses of his face when I dared raise my head, his shadow dancing in my lap, twisting as he moved.

And beneath him, I rocked with the tempo, my own body throbbing, sensitive, unmoored.

"Touch yourself," he said suddenly, watching me, pivoting his legs. "Have you ever done that before, while thinking of me?"

I couldn't answer, but as I unclasped my belt, my grip tight against my own skin, Bren swore in response, nearly losing himself on my tongue.

"Fuck," he said again, and he grinned, flashing all his teeth. "I bet you have. Gods, will you focus on you? Let me watch."

So I did, lowering my other hand from where I'd been holding him by the waist, and above me, Bren set a pace that was agonizingly slow, his hips angled back so he could see me, mesmerized, his gaze on the flash of my fingers.

And there, beneath him, I was trembling too, as hard in my hand as he was in my mouth. It overwhelmed me, to have him like this, and to feel that burning need for relief in my own body, from my own touch, building higher and higher.

I groaned. Even with my mouth full, my lips around him, the sound snuck past me, surprising me. I pulled back, shifting away from him, but just long enough to breathe.

Then I came, and it was blinding, the way I felt. And Bren stiffened, overcome with it, before he shuddered too.

I took a moment, sitting a little further back in the grass, distracted, drunk. But then Bren jerked against my mouth, desperate, helpless.

So I let him have this—have *me*.

"I'm yours," I said, and he nodded, pleased.

Bren fucked me, then, at exactly the pace he wanted, thrusting against my lips in a quick, almost greedy tempo that only narrowly avoided my teeth. And I enjoyed it, keeping up, rocking with him until he circled the edge and murmured my name.

"Keenyn, you don't—" he started to say, but I held still, urging him to let go.

And with no other warning, Bren lost himself in a

sudden, high burst of sound, filling all the space around us just for a moment, loud and brief. Then he stifled the cry, shuddering against me again and again, until his grip on my hair finally loosened, going slack.

I swallowed around him, feeling him soften, then pulled myself away from his body and away from his feet. "You okay?" I asked, and in a flash of doubt, added, "Was that okay?"

And in response, Bren moved his hand along my jaw, then tipped up my chin, as I hoped he would. I'd grown used to it, craving that control, and he liked to take it.

"Look at me," he said, and I did. Our eyes met again, and there was magic there, comforting and close.

Then he leaned all the way down to kiss me, and I smiled, warm against his mouth.

CHAPTER ELEVEN

In that long, quiet hour before dawn, while Bren and I were still alone; in the gentle, lingering warmth of what came after, when the road to Warrenhall was still gloomy and dark; we rode slowly, carefully, his hips in my hands, smiling at the shared realization that all our secrets had turned out to be the same.

"I still can't believe you didn't know," he said, and when he glanced back to meet my eyes, his body twisting in the saddle, I was reminded of how tightly he'd held me, how fiercely he'd kissed me, and how passionate he'd been.

A surge of heat rose to my cheeks. "There were days I thought you hated me," I admitted, my voice low as I cleared my throat. And his reaction, to how bewildered I looked, was a simple shake of his head.

~

To avoid the temptation of going any further, here, on the side of the road, we agreed not to reach for each other, and to separate once we dismounted. But even still, with our horse turned toward a nearby stream, our boots planted solidly a few paces apart, Bren caught my wrist, the cold bite of his metal gauntlet keeping space between us, forced and strange.

"I have one thing to say," he whispered, "and I'll let it go."

I turned away from him, my eyes on the edge of the horizon, trying to ignore how red his ears had gone. "It's rarely one thing, when it comes to you," I said.

In reply, his laugh was husky, unsteady. "Don't change your mind before we get back to Warrenhall," he said. "It's all I can think about. How I'm going to throw those pretty little hips of yours on the best bed we can afford and take you *apart.*"

Hearing that, my body reacted to the closeness, to the promise, by shivering.

"You're impossible," I said, and purposefully drew out our waterskins, dodging the touch of his lips, searching and needy, on the edge of my cheek. "You know exactly what you're doing."

"I do," he said, suddenly serious. And I meant to laugh, but with my heart still racing, my pulse high, I slipped partway down the slight embankment to the water instead, the grass slick with mud. And for that single moment, I lost sight of him, his hair a flash of gold in the sunlight.

Cursing, I glanced at my hand, my palm torn open by the rough bark of the tree that had broken my fall. I turned back, expecting to see him smirking, but instead, the long stretch of road behind me was empty.

"Bren?" I said.

But then the faintest sound of shuffling caught my attention in the undergrowth on my right.

Reaching for one of my swords, I kept it low, the tip

angled towards the undergrowth. But as soon as I noticed it, the movement died, and the leaves grew still.

There was a long, hollow beat of silence.

Then nothing, as if the world was holding its breath.

After a moment, feeling the tiniest pinprick of relief, I sighed. Overreacting was one thing, and as I stepped forward, tentative, paranoid—

Something shot out, violent and quick, grabbing my ankle.

With a start, I fell forward, and the shape of a figure crawled suddenly out of the ground in a mass of worms, dark soil, and black flesh. It was thinner than any human, emaciated and dead, with long limbs and bony hands, its face a mask of mushrooms and death.

It lunged, then, before I could speak, before I could *yell*, its black limbs and scarred mouth swinging out at me with gleaming teeth, snapping at my leg. I dodged by rolling backwards, into the stream, but only just managed to avoid being struck by another bony hand, reaching out of the mud, grabbing at my head and arms.

Each claw-like finger, long and black, whistled past me, jabbing at my face as if to pierce straight through my eye. I turned, just in time, but I felt the burn along my ear. It clipped me, slicing the skin and spilling blood into the freezing water.

I gasped at the nearness, at the shock of it, twisting away as I scrambled for the grass, but another creature lunged out of nowhere, its body covered with rotting, peeling skin, its mouth marred by mud.

I parried with my drawn blade, gouging through soft veins that poured black blood onto my boots. But every- where I looked, everywhere I stepped, another creature seemed to rip itself from the soil, moving in an explosion of bone and rock.

With a start, I cried out, "Bren, by the stream!" But as I spoke, the nearest creature slashed at me with broken fingernails, sharpened to points, while another bit down hard on my leg, careering out of the water to eat me alive.

I started stabbing at them wildly, swinging as high as I dared. In glimpses, I saw beneath their bony exteriors and found organs, shrivelled and dead, hanging like sacks of flesh in a bird cage.

At last, one strike hit true, and the third creature, biting at my leg, reared back at the impact of my blade. But at the same time, the first creature swung its head forward and smashed into my nose. I twisted again, trying to keep hold of my sword, but saw only stars and reddish-black spots as I pulled away.

Gritting my teeth, my mouth full of blood, I made a choice. A bad one.

Already, I was completely surrounded, and it was *quiet* —only these monsters' gnawing teeth made any sound, dull and muffled by their swollen tongues. And still, I'd heard nothing of Bren—and that *terrified* me.

So I rushed toward the creature on my right, slashing deftly at its bony head, and when it swung both hands high to try and block the blow, I ran past it, seeing my opening in the throng of bodies.

It could very well have grabbed me as I passed or bitten me again with its sharp row of grimy teeth, but I kept running. I had to.

Bursting out onto the wider expanse of the road, blood running over my lips and down my chin, I found five of the same skeletal creatures standing around Bren, two of them grappling with him from behind, their long arms wrapped around his throat like rope. The others were stabbing at him with their hands, uncaring that their bony fingers met his breastplate over and over again, denting the metal.

Immediately, I charged into the fray, stepping over a pile of splintered bodies next to where his sword had fallen in the road. I struck him in the side, with my shoulder, knocking him and the two figures behind him into the dirt, then heard him gasp, his eyes red, his throat bloody, as both his hands flew to the dark rings that circled his neck.

An instant later, the two creatures I'd knocked down scrambled to their feet, and the other three, still standing, plunged forward again, stabbing their long fingers and blunt knuckles at our legs and backs, their bloody teeth snapping at our faces.

But Bren moved faster, so fast I hardly followed the movement. And with his hands around me, he flipped us over, taking the blows himself, horrific and deep, into his shoulders and thighs. I felt the tips of those bony fingers like needles against my skin, piercing straight through him.

Then we jerked apart, Bren's muffled shout of pain swallowed by the cries of the three, six, ten—no, *twelve* creatures that had followed me from the stream, now crowding all around us on the road, their faces perfect mirrors, their empty eye sockets as dark and grotesque as their exposed ribs.

Bren bought us time, grabbing his blade and swinging it wildly, his coughs ragged, his chest heaving, blood spilling down his neck and over his breastplate. It looked like they'd tried to behead him, the lines grim, the gashes deep, and with another dozen wounds in his back, it was a miracle he was standing at all.

I thought to heal him—and I reached out, meaning to—but to touch him for long enough would surely get us both killed. And the creatures had already surrounded us again, twenty becoming thirty, then forty, then fifty, as an entire battalion of long-dead bodies broke free from the dirt, slashing with their open hands like their fingers were refined, steel weapons, wanton in their rage.

And still, even when I split one creature's skull, Bren's sword carving through the spine of another, they continued lashing out from the ground, their teeth tearing through our boots, their dead hearts beating almost audibly in the crisp, morning air.

It was too much.

Bren's next strike, wide and cutting, broke through a line of them, but he nearly impaled me on the backswing, his attacks too hasty, too uncoordinated, his massive blade catching the reflection of his cloak, torn and blue, in the metal.

I yelped, ducking below his sword, twisting away from another creature, only to stand again and take a strike directly to the shoulder. The weapon, a severed arm, had been broken at the elbow like a wooden spear shaft, the sharp end driving me backwards into a tree.

The pain was excruciating, numbed only by shock. I made no sound, only opened my mouth to scream, before that same creature shoved its entire body weight against its arm, pushing the broken bone entirely through my body and into the bark behind me. With a shudder, I dropped my sword, my left arm going completely numb.

"Bren!" I cried out, kicking at the creature as it grabbed at my face, its raised hand only inches from gouging out my eyes. "Seven gods, help me!"

But Bren didn't respond, my view of him blocked by the mass of bodies that swarmed all around us. In his silence, another creature lunged up out of the ground and stabbed me, its hand plunging into my chest.

I felt the moment those horrid, jagged fingers broke my ribs, ripping through my skin and my fighting leathers like they were hardly in the way. I saw stars in my eyes, my vision flooded with pain, and it was only my instincts, acting without conscious thought, that saved me from taking another mouthful of snapping teeth to the thigh.

I looked up quickly, past the two creatures pinning me down, and finally found Bren, his cloak the only flash of colour beneath the mountain of bodies, some moving, some still, another creature behind him, pulling at his neck, biting at his exposed skin.

I had never felt terror like this before. Another heart-beat passed and I watched as Bren fell to his knees, the mottled leaves beneath his body only darkening, his blood running black in the twisting shadows cast by the horde of monsters.

Seeing him stumble, collapse, stole all the breath from me.

I stopped thinking.

I have to save him.

With a sharp cry, I grabbed the bone stabbed through my shoulder and pulled it free with a strangled shout. My left arm was useless, my nose still bleeding over my teeth, but I smashed my head into the mouth of the creature with its hand in my chest, pushing it away, just as golden light flared out against my skin, my broken nose and shattered bones stitching themselves back together. Then, just as I leapt to the side, atop a heap of broken bodies, I drew my other sword.

Quickly, manically, I jabbed at the creature in front of me with the flat of my hand, then spun my blade and punctured its head. Then I flared my magic, my other hand grabbing its face, and coloured the lines of its shattered bones with a blast of golden light, viciously rending its skull apart.

Ignoring the draw I felt on my body, the exhaustion like a physical loss, I dodged another lunge out of the shadows, the flash of black bone, broken in two places, cutting into a low-hanging branch. And when a reaching hand circled my boot, I stabbed it with my sword, swinging high with my right hand afterwards and plunging my blade into another skull before dodging a snapping jaw meant to rip through my arm.

All the while, I felt the cost of the magic drag at my hands, making my heart rate and my breathing unsteady, even as I smashed my elbow into another creature's face, heard its nose crack, its body shudder, and filled its face with gold.

I stepped back, wiping blood from my mouth with the back of my hand, then threw my dagger, the blade whistling through the air before it struck the creature behind Bren, the impact breaking its face in two, its body crumpling onto the grass.

But Bren fell too, face-first into the road, and I felt all the hope leave my body in a single, shaking gasp.

There were only a handful of those creatures left now, the rest cleaved apart by Bren's sword or under my golden, reckless hands, but I stopped being able to see them clearly. I beheaded them carelessly, one by one, yelling into the air as I moved with a sloppiness that would've gotten me killed ten minutes before, when there'd been more.

"Bren," I said, because he was all that mattered. All that had ever mattered.

Weightless, drained, I watched as the last creature dropped back into the overturned earth, all the adrenaline leaving my body in a rush, my limbs locking in place. Using my magic like this had cost me so much, but if I collapsed now...

No. I closed my eyes. Centred myself. Breathed. "Bren?" I called again, waiting for a reply, my voice shaking. "Bren, I can't—"

I pushed myself. Forced myself. Step by step, I jerked my body another foot or two towards him, unwilling to believe the truth that was laid bare before my eyes.

Bren's face was turned away from me, the usual sounds of the forest around us completely absent. There was a hiss of the wind, from somewhere far in the distance, but that only made the hush of the open road all the worse.

Slowly, my vision began to fill with black spots and white lines. It started in the middle, spreading outwards like a ripple in a pond. In a moment, I'd go blind, my organs shutting down one by one.

With a groan, I dropped to my knees, and put my hand on Bren's head. It was slick with warm blood, but still solid to the touch.

There was no grace to this—to saving him. Or trying to. I grabbed his shoulder and heaved him towards me, turning his body, trying to break his fall as he thumped back against the dirt. But here, in full view, everything about his injuries looked worse. His face was ashen, and his throat was threaded with dark, horrific bruising. I wasn't sure if he was breathing, and I was shaking too much to check.

My entire body was starting to go numb, the weakness spreading out from my legs. I had saved myself from dying in the mouth of a monster, but had resigned myself to collapsing here, from magic-induced exhaustion. From overextending. From trying to be enough, and failing.

I leaned forward. I couldn't keep myself upright anymore. Gingerly, I touched Bren's face.

He was still warm. And in the dazzling sunlight, his expression seemed almost peaceful, his lips slightly parted, his eyes closed, his cheeks flushed. His face would be the last I'd ever see, and I'd never hated myself more. Hated myself for wasting so much time.

I lowered my head against his chest, wanting to be near him, needing to sleep, to rest, to *give in*. But for either of us to have a chance of surviving this, one of us would have to be conscious. Awake. Aware.

I could only see out of the corners of my eyes now, but I could feel my fingertips, and I knew I was still touching Bren's face.

I could make no other choice.

I closed my eyes, praying quickly, softly, in elvish.

Then I pulled on every last reserve that I had, reaching deep inside my chest, hollowing myself out, flaring magic into my hands.

I saw a flicker of light through my eyelids, the warmth like a sun, familiar but distant. *This* would surely kill me, if anything would.

I knew pouring whatever of my magic remained into Bren's broken body was a fool's choice, but I gritted my teeth and did it anyway.

I wouldn't lose him. Not like this.

CHAPTER TWELVE

With no understanding of the time that had passed, I woke up stiff and sore with my head on a pillow, Bren's body sprawled awkwardly across me in a shared, narrow bed. It creaked as I moved, filling the world with too much sound. Then my breath rushed back to me like I'd gasped after choking, my head clearing before my eyes did, the spots in my vision hiding more of the room from me until I blinked.

Gradually, as I settled, the darkness peeled back to reveal a small space with a wooden door and a white ceiling. It was cold, but only because my body was numb; as I moved, trying to wiggle out from under Bren, feeling came back to my skin in starts and bursts, revealing how sticky and sweaty I was in my borrowed, scratchy clothes. I recognized nothing—not where I was, what I was wearing, or how I'd come to be here. The only anchor in the room was Bren, who slept like a dead horse.

In his defence, he looked unbelievably comfortable; he was lying diagonally across my body, his head by the wall and his hips over my legs, his feet sticking out over the end of the bed. And he was snoring, his face slightly pink, his forehead creased. Whatever he was dreaming about, it consumed him.

Gently, afraid I would wake him, I slid myself towards the floor and eased onto the threadbare excuse for a rug. It was dirty, dusty, and smelled like mildew, but I hardly cared.

I just needed a mouthful of water. Anything to soothe my horribly scratchy throat, dry mouth, and seemingly swollen tongue.

Finding one of Bren's waterskins atop a pile of my folded clothes, armour, and weapons, I drank deeply. And despite how stale the water tasted, I kept swallowing it, the relief spreading from my neck to my hands and beyond. It grounded me, even as my body started to violently shake.

I felt hungry, hollowed out, and weak. I felt tired, confused, and every inch of my chest hurt. For a moment, I let that distract me.

Anything was easier than confronting the truth. That I had survived. And that somehow, I'd done enough to save Bren.

It was a strange feeling, and I wasn't entirely sure why it wasn't euphoric. Instead, I felt weighed down by it, belittled. I didn't regret my choice, in the end, but the horror of it, the terror I'd grappled with—it ruined me. Doubling over, I hugged myself, exhausted by the mere idea of being alive.

This was the closest I'd ever come to death. The closest I'd ever come to watching Bren die. The realization made me gag, but there was nothing in my body to spit up except for the water I'd just swallowed.

I couldn't remember any of it. Only the darkness, just before I woke; the numbness; the long stretch of feeling nothing and knowing nothing. Was that what death was like? Being unable to fight, only to close your eyes and let go?

Overwhelmed, I sat down on the ground and leaned back on my hands, feeling the stretch in my legs as they strained with the effort of any movement at all. In this dark, tiny room, I felt like I existed outside of time; I could only breathe, center myself, and settle.

Then, after a long moment, I regained control of my raging thoughts and forced myself to focus on what was still in front of me: Bren. A man who, in all honesty, I cared about a lot more than I ever let on.

Between this job and the last, everything had changed between us. We'd gone from grumbling monster hunters to...whatever we were now. Whatever this was.

The word came to me. *Lovers?*

It was strange to think about.

Easing back onto the edge of the bed, I reached out and pushed my hand through his hair, his gentle blond curls clinging to my fingertips as he stirred, leaning towards me. "Mm?" he said, the question not really sound. It was mostly meant as a feeling, passing from his mouth to mine as he turned his head toward me, pulling me in for a kiss.

We didn't speak; we just held each other, loose and careful, his featherlight touches across my chest exceedingly gentle. He was mindful of my injuries, trailing his fingers under my shirt and along the delicate white cloth that was bound around my shoulder and over my ribs. In turn, I traced the lines and curves of his body, looking for something real—the beat of his heart, the rise and fall of his breath.

Finally, in the softest voice, he said, "Don't ever do that again."

"Do what?" I replied, smiling just a little against his mouth. "Save your life? Share a bed with you?"

He shook his head, a little bemused, and then pulled me into a hug, dragging me further onto the bed and partially over his body. "Almost die," he clarified, his eyes blinking as he pushed away what remained of the veil of sleep. "It's been over two weeks. Your heart stopped beating more than once."

Avoiding his gaze, I sighed heavily, hating the sound of the agony I heard in his voice. I could tell from how little he'd shaved, how soundly he'd slept, and how dark the bags were under his eyes that he'd hardly taken a moment for himself since what happened. Watching me waste away, powerless to help, must have been its own kind of torture.

"At least we're alive," I said, offering the words like they'd console him. "I'm sorry though. It must've been a hard ride, getting back here."

Bren lifted his hands in response, tenderly cupping the sides of my face as he spoke. "I carried you here," he said. "We lost the horse. It was all I could do."

I tried not to imagine it. "Then I'm doubly sorry."

Looking more serious than I usually saw him, Bren's eyes moved from my mouth to my left shoulder, no doubt staring through my clothes again as if he could see the bandaged wounds beneath. "The healing mages here aren't as powerful as you," he said. "You might actually scar."

At that, I laughed. "We'll match, then."

With a smile, Bren paused, allowing a natural lull to break the conversation. Then he pulled me forward again, holding me gently as I relaxed against his chest. I liked listening to him breathe, his palms warm against my back. But he never stopped moving, his fingers following the lines along my shoulders and my waist, tracing the dips and the turns like he was trying to memorize every last one. He was rarely so contemplative.

"Share your thoughts with me?" I asked him, when the quiet stretched on too long.

Bren met my gaze, something inside him finally breaking. "I thought I'd lost you," he said, and the words fell out of him with the force of every day we'd been apart. "I thought—"

He trailed off, holding me tighter, squeezing.

"Please," he murmured. "Don't ever put me through that again. I'd rather die than be without you."

Whatever this was—this emotion, this *desperation* from him—I barely survived it.

"I love you too," I said softly. "I'm sorry I scared you."

It was all I could say. And for a while, we stayed like that, just him and I, until he'd composed himself enough to speak.

"What do we do now?" he asked, his lips in my hair. "Take another job? Head back to the capital?"

I wasn't sure, but I was ready to find out. "Are you feeling better? Can you fight?"

At that, Bren snorted, then leaned further back on the pillow we shared. In the dim light, coming in from under the door, I could see his neck had only a single band of bruising and discolouration. "You healed most of it," he said. "This is all that's left. Though I very nearly had my throat torn out."

I closed my eyes. "I thought I'd lost you too," I said, whispering into the darkness. "I've never seen you so still, or so badly wounded."

Shifting his arm out from under me, Bren tipped up my chin, prompting me to meet his gaze. He was partially sitting up now, leaning on his elbow, and I moved my legs between his, tangling us together.

"Why did you kiss me?" he asked softly, running his thumb over my lips. "That first time, in the forest. Why did you ask?"

I furrowed my brow. "What do you mean?"

I knew, of course. I just wanted to hear him say it.

"We've been working together for nearly a decade," he replied, "and you've never once looked at me like that. With interest. Like you wanted more than what we had."

"I adore you," I replied honestly. "I have for a long time. I just...didn't know those feelings could be romantic. Until now."

Pulling away, I sat up on the bed, my back against the headboard, crossing my legs so I could still lean over and kiss him if I wanted to. "It's complicated."

Bren grunted. "What changed, then? Why now?"

Sensing he needed the truth, I shrugged. "I had a dream about you," I said, and surprisingly, I didn't feel at all embarrassed or ashamed. I trusted Bren; we'd established that this was what we both wanted. So the origin didn't inherently matter. "I guess I hadn't really *looked* at you before then. Not like that. But once I had, there was no going back."

"A dream?" Bren said, but this time, he asked the question with a smirk. "Was it the morning you slept in late? During the storm? You wouldn't meet my eyes for some time."

Thinking back on it now, I flushed. "I can't deny that, Bren."

There was a long beat of silence, before slowly, deliberately, Bren moved forward and kissed me. He had such a dominating presence, even half-naked in a tiny bed in a dark room, his arms and chest bare. It was like he was everywhere, surrounding me, the heat of him enveloping my skin.

"I would've taken you to bed years ago, if you'd let me," he said. "You're impossible not to admire."

I shook my head. "Seven gods. A genuine compliment? I must be dead."

But again, instead of smiling, Bren just pulled me down against him, falling silent. Then he eased me backwards, onto the sheets, my head on the pillow. I didn't resist, but kept him close. On my back, he caged me in, his one arm supporting his head as he hovered just above me.

"You took me by surprise, in the woods," he said. "But I was selfish then. Excited. I'd long since written off that you'd ever think of me this way."

Impulsively, I pulled at the strings that held his trousers around his waist. He didn't stop me.

"And now what?" I asked, breathing the question into the curves of his lips, into the inch of darkness that separated us.

"Now I want whatever you want," he said, his eyes pinning me down, his voice smooth and steady. "And I won't ask for anything more than that. Wherever you lead, I'll follow."

"But is that *all* you want?"

Bren hummed against my neck, kissing me there, then again by my ear. "I want to be everything we need," he said, admitting it like a confession, even as his cheeks turned red. "I want to spoil you enough that you'll come back. That you'll want more of me, like this."

Heat pooled in my stomach, watching as Bren shimmied out of his clothes and settled into the bed next to me. I closed my eyes again, knowing at once what I wanted, needing only to have heard that Bren wanted the same.

"You'd have to be absolutely terrible at this," I said, "to convince me I only want one night with you."

Bren smiled, and in the darkness, his face was like the sun. "Good," he said softly. "Because there's a thousand things I can't wait to do."

CHAPTER THIRTEEN

I had expected my first time with Bren to be rough. A moment of passion, spontaneity, with both of us standing, his arms holding me up. But none of that ended up being true. Instead, Bren moved slowly, making sure I was comfortable before his hand slipped below my waist and beneath my clothes, his pace suiting the quiet, careful moment we'd carved out between us, even as we both shivered from the closeness.

Lightly—agonizingly so—he ran his palm down the length of me, teasing out a reaction. I groaned, hardening under his touch, smothering the sound against his lips.

"You have to keep quiet," he murmured, twisting closer to my side, kissing me with half his mouth. "We're not the only ones here in the healing house."

I nodded, only half-listening, and he smirked again. Then he finally stroked me, tentatively, just once. I closed my eyes, swallowing back another groan, my fingers itching to touch him just as he was touching me, though he asked me not to.

"Just enjoy it," he said, and he tightened his grip a bit

more, gauging how I trembled, before he pulled away and spit in his hand.

"Slower?" he asked, still taking his time, seizing my lips again with his own. His mouth was hot, his tongue insistent, but he didn't push anything. Didn't hurry.

"You're a menace," I whispered back, echoing what he'd said in the woods, and he smiled as I reached for his shoulder, tracing the faint lines of the pale, white scars there. "Don't make me beg."

In response, he dropped his hand, moving his fingers between my legs. The pressure was gentle, the touch exploratory, but the absence of him, where he'd been before, made me *ache*.

"Bren," I said, and the plea was more breath than sound. I lost track of the room, of the creaking wooden bed, of my body, and just breathed into his hair, tangling my fingers behind his head. "I want it faster. *Please*."

He grinned, triumphant in all the best ways, even as I saw a flush of colour spread across his cheeks. Then, I felt him stir against my thigh, stiffening with the slightest friction, and I reached for him.

It was only for a moment, with my head still on the pillow, my hand around the length of him. I caught his bottom lip between my teeth, and he stilled, giving in, enjoying the bite as I stroked him in tandem.

But then he pushed my hand away, using his right arm and his body weight to hold me in place, catching my wrist as I tried to snake my palm further between us, to tease a little more tension from him. "Take your clothes off, then," he said, leaning over me. "If you're so impatient."

I couldn't have done it faster. With one hand, I shimmied out of the restraint of my shirt and my pants, pushing everything down to the end of the bed.

Bren made an appreciative sound, though he'd seen me naked a thousand times before. Then he kissed me again, our teeth bumping together.

"You've had other lovers," he said, and though he'd never asked me, he assumed the truth. "Would you see them again?"

I watched his expression, the way his gaze slid from mine, his eyes on my chest. "That's not a real question," I replied. "Ask me what you want to know."

He smiled, and with the barest, upward shift of his brow, he said, "Will you tell me what they've done? What you like?"

I could barely breathe from how badly I wanted him, just then. So I moved my knees, and he settled immediately into the space between my thighs, our bodies rubbing together, a surge of pleasure slipping down my throat.

I groaned. I couldn't help it. He looked glorious, spread above me like this, his arms pinning me against the bed.

"You're the only one," I said honestly, watching as he pressed a trail of kisses down my chest, the anticipation of his mouth on that urgent, intimate part of me driving me mad. "There's no one else. I don't take strangers to bed."

Bren paused, his tongue at the base of me, wet and greedy. I had to look away from him; the intensity of his gaze made my breath catch.

"Ah," he said simply, his expression careful, guarded. Then he smirked, breathing out against me, and I jerked in his hands. "We'll just have to see what you enjoy, then, won't we?"

In a single movement, far from graceful, Bren took me in his mouth, sliding his tongue over my skin, and I nearly shouted.

I had the perfect view—his lips were red, almost pink,

and when I shuddered, he took me deeper, until I thought he might swallow me. I craned my head, getting moment-to-moment glimpses of myself sliding in and out of him, his mouth ruthless as he moved with me, restless as his hands had been.

Trying to stay together, to stay whole, was the hardest part. I covered my mouth with my wrist, biting the skin to muffle the moans, but still the sounds slipped out of me in gasps and starts, my knees lifting off the bed. And Bren made it worse, his hands heavy on my thighs, trying to keep me within reach of him.

Desperate, I grabbed his hair, needing something to hold, something to pull, something to ground myself. But as I did, he moaned too, shaking with the pleasure of it, his eyes snapping shut.

Seeing that, my hips bucked against his mouth, and when he pulled back, he took me in his hand again, stroking faster than before. Then he angled himself higher, partially over my chest, supporting himself on his elbow.

He gestured with the fingers of his free hand, and I immediately understood.

"Gods, please," I stuttered, feeling myself begin to crest. "Go."

Throwing my legs over his shoulders, I let him have me, eager and willing, as my body shook with the force of how hard I came. And though he expected it, Bren still made a small sound of surprise, my pleasure painting his chest, the colour a sharp contrast against his skin.

"Fuck," he murmured, his eyes on my face. "That suits you. The expression you make."

I could hardly respond, the relief mixing with a renewed sense of neediness as he kept moving, the pressure building, his fingers slick with something cold he'd spilled onto his hand. "I like yours too," I breathed out. "How pleasure changes you."

Bren stifled a shy laugh, then shifted out from between my legs so he could kiss me again, the moment sloppy. Then he hesitated, his body bent over me, his voice shaking. "I have to be careful here," he told me softly. "I'm...much stronger than you."

"You won't break me," I replied, kissing him back, kissing him harder. "I'll be vocal, though."

Bren smiled, aligning his body and withdrawing his hand. "Just talk to me," he said, and he eased himself forward, taking me.

Immediately, I felt myself tense all around him, around that first half inch of him, and I grabbed his arm. He stilled, then moved gingerly, pushing in only a hairsbreadth at a time, pausing often. He made the entry about me, though his body shook, and mine trembled.

"Gods," Bren said, and he pressed a kiss to my shoulder, his hips nearly flush against mine. I started to relax, the pressure easing, but I was breathless. "Keenyn, I—"

"Don't," I said, cutting him off, shifting my legs, sighing beneath him. "I'm all right. I like the feeling of you."

He shuddered again, his next exhale a sharp sound that caught in his teeth as I urged the movement of his hips, trying to guide him, and he matched my pace.

Closing my eyes, I fell into the slow, steady rhythm of his body meeting mine, the sensation shooting through me, my legs shaking against his knees. And I found myself enjoying it, that slide of him, animalistic and raw, as he pushed inside me over and over.

As he grew more confident, he went faster, his elbows digging into the bed. "Fuck," he said, and I felt the sting, the urgency, as he started to lose himself. Lose control. "Gods, you're a gift."

At last, my body aching with each solid thrust, he began to unravel. His eyes couldn't focus, so he shut them, another moan slipping off his tongue.

"Keenyn," he said, bending forward, my name a tangled mess.

I grabbed his hair, remembering what he liked, and pulled him undone.

Bren came with a shudder, his last couple of thrusts sloppy and shallow, holding me as he mumbled something incoherent under his breath. Then he kissed me again, before wrapping his arms around my chest and burying his nose in my hair.

In the silence, afterward, I pulled him into the bed, easing him against the pillow. He let me hold him by the waist, his body warm and sticky between my arms. "I'm still here," I teased, kissing the side of his mouth, then curling closer to him. Gods, he was beautiful like this, his expression satisfied and sleepy.

Bren opened his eyes, drinking me in, his grip around my chest tightening until he held us together, hip to hip. Any tighter, and he'd break one of my ribs.

Then, like the words hadn't come from him, Bren whispered, "I love you. I've loved you since the day I met you. You know that, don't you?"

His admission settled where there was no space between us. Where every part of our bodies met, his chest to my chest, my hand to his heart.

I hadn't needed to hear him say it, but the sound of the words, serious and sentimental, did something to what was already trapped inside me, easing a tightness I hadn't known was there, until there was no tightness at all.

I smiled. "I will go wherever you take me," I said, in elvish, like I had on the night he'd asked me to run away with him, to abandon my claim to the throne, to desert. Then, changing tongues, I said it again, and pressed the next few words against the warmth of his cheek. "You are half of my soul."

In response, Bren squeezed my hand, and never let go.

ACKNOWLEDGMENTS

Writing this book was a labour of love four years in the making, and I'm forever grateful to the people in my life who supported me every step of the way.

To my sister, Katie: thank you for loving me dearly, even when I was finding myself. You're my sweet pea, my honey-bee, and I'm glad we'll always have each other.

To my brother, Matthew: thank you for always having my back and hearing me out. You're everything everyone wishes their brother could be, and more.

To my father: thank you for inspiring my love of reading and for being my rock whenever I lose my way. I hope I never stop making you proud.

To my mother: thank you for always encouraging me and for holding my life together when I can't anymore. You make every trip an adventure, and I'm so lucky to be your daughter.

To the Penguins—Maddy, Laura, Melissa, and Yianna: thank you for more than sixty years of combined friendship, and for our weekly calls. The pandemic wouldn't have been as survivable without you.

To Bolton: thank you for being my absolutely incredible, endlessly patient, and immeasurably talented audiobook narrator. You not only changed the way I see this book, but my outlook on audio storytelling as a whole. Working with you has been a highlight of my life.

To Reid, my visionary of a cover artist: thank you for

creating the most perfect illustration of Keenyn and Bren I'll ever know. Your cover art is truly a gift.

To Ren, Elizabeth, and Leslie: thank you for your expertise and care with the book's typography and formatting. It takes a village, and you were mine.

And finally, to Nick: thank you for believing in me even when *I* didn't believe in me. Without you, I'd likely be sitting in a quiet corner somewhere, writing books about small towns that have multiple bus routes, and truly, that would be a travesty.

Thank you. Thank you. Thank you.

ABOUT THE AUTHOR

Amanda Ferreira works in publishing, as an editor. She lives in Toronto with her tuxedo cat, Milo, and when not writing, can be found baking, running, listening to a true crime podcast, or working on a cosplay.

Connect with her on Twitter (@amandatferreira) or Instagram (@aferreirawrites) for updates on her next book.

www.ingramcontent.com/pod-product-compliance
Lightning Source LLC
Chambersburg PA
CBHW030236180626
46810CB00008B/3150